STRANGE POSSESSION

**Center Point
Large Print**

**This Large Print Book carries the
Seal of Approval of N.A.V.H.**

STRANGE
POSSESSION

Dorothy Garlock

CENTER POINT PUBLISHING
THORNDIKE, MAINE

This Center Point Large Print edition
is published in the year 2009 by arrangement with
Grand Central Publishing,
a division of Hachette Book Group, USA.

Copyright © 1982 by Johanna Phillips.

The text of this Large Print edition is unabridged.
In other aspects, this book may vary
from the original edition.
Printed in the United States of America.
Set in 16-point Times New Roman type.

ISBN: 978-1-60285-418-5

B+T   32.95   7/09

Library of Congress Cataloging-in-Publication Data

Garlock, Dorothy.
  Strange possession / Dorothy Garlock.
     p. cm.
  ISBN 978-1-60285-418-5 (library binding : alk. paper)
  1. Large type books. I. Title.

PS3557.A71645S77 2009
813'.54--dc22

2008047594

To Betty O'Haver
sister, friend . . . lovely lady

CHAPTER ONE

THE SMELL OF burning spruce aroused her.

She lay with her eyes closed, feigning sleep. A clatter of iron told her that Mike was satisfied with the blaze in the fireplace and had moved to the big cooking range that dominated the other end of the room. Kelly opened her eyes a crack. He was pouring water from a granite bucket into the reservoir on the side of the range.

The strangeness of it all hit her. Here she was, in this spruce log cabin, deep in the wilderness, two hundred miles north of Anchorage, and she had not felt even a scrap of fright when she was awakened out of a sound sleep by someone moving about the cabin.

How different from Boston and the security-patrolled building where she had lived for eight months. The elegant, marble-floored apartment, its furniture spotlessly maintained, the vases of fresh flowers, arranged and placed in just the right places—somehow it had all seemed unreal.

After the first two months in her Boston home, Kelly should have settled into her new life, but the tension grew daily until she and her husband Jack were living like two hostile strangers. They pretended conjugal bliss in public, but they barely spoke to each other in private.

Jack. Oh, how his sister hated to hear Jonathan

Winslow Templeton the Third called . . . Jack! Kelly could see her now, sitting in regal splendor behind the silver coffee service, every hair in place, her critical eyes looking over Kelly's own unruly black hair. The long, slim fingers knew just the right touch on the ornate, silver bell to summon the maid, who would enter the room like a robot, the smooth, discreet carpeting silencing her steps, her black uniform and crisp apron making her a shadow to be ignored. According to Katherine Templeton Hathorn, one didn't smile at a maid or acknowledge her presence as a person.

Katherine had never made any secret of her feelings about the girl her brother had met in Anchorage and married shortly after. To her, Kelly simply did not measure up to the Templeton standards. Katherine was forty-eight, had been married briefly and acquired a stepdaughter, Nancy. Now widowed, her main goal in life was to unite her brother and her stepdaughter in marriage. Kelly had been quite a setback to those plans.

Lazily Kelly opened her eyes and found herself looking directly at a dark window. Night had come quickly. She turned on her back, stretching luxuriously, pleasantly tired and relaxed. She was home! Home, in the wilderness of Alaska, where she had lived since she was ten years old.

After her mother had died fourteen years ago, she and her father had come here. He had built the main room of this cabin with his own hands. Later he had added two bedrooms and built two other cabins to rent out to hunters, as well as the main lodge they used to house winter skiers or people who came to ride snowmobiles on the trails around Mount McKinley. The tourist business had been good since the Anchorage–Fairbanks highway had been completed. They even had electricity now, which made available conveniences they had gotten used to doing without.

Kelly switched on a lamp, and sat up, rubbing her stocking feet on the thick fur rug on the floor. She surveyed the room. Everything was dusty, mousey, and in disorder. Cobwebs swayed like darkened moss in the gentle draft created by the half-open fireplace chimney. Well, what did she expect? she scolded herself. The resort had been closed since her father had died two years ago. Mike had been living here alone since Marty, his twin sister, had taken a job in Fairbanks. No doubt his cabin was spotless. This one would have been too, if she'd let him know she was coming.

Mike and Marty had lived here almost as long as Kelly. They had arrived with their mother in response to an advertisement for a cook that Kelly's father had placed in the paper. Aunt Mary had been the nearest thing to a mother Kelly had ever known, as her own mother had been ill for many years before she died. Kelly had often wondered why her father never married Aunt Mary. She was sure he loved her. Only after her death did she discover why: Aunt Mary had a husband. A worthless man, who had never contributed to the support of his family, but, nevertheless, a husband. Kelly's father was as fond of Mike and Marty as if they were his own children, and when he died he left half of his estate to them and the other half to Kelly.

Five years ago Kelly had gone to Anchorage to work. Her father approved of her reason for getting away from the resort. Mike was in love with her. Kelly knew she would never feel anything more for him than sisterly love and it hurt her unbearably to see the look of longing in Mike's eyes when she turned suddenly to see him watching her. The whole situation made her want to weep. But out of sight, out of mind, she reasoned. Her job with the newspaper was interesting and on long weekends she could catch the train and be home in less than six hours. She made friends in Anchorage, but none as close as Mike and Marty. When her father died suddenly, it was a shock to them all. Mike had been working as a lineman for the utility company and they decided to close down the resort for the time being.

Four months after her father's funeral, Kelly met Jack. She literally ran him down as she made a dash to the office with her advertising copy. They collided with such force that she was almost flung to the sidewalk. Jack grabbed her and held her until she regained her balance. Then he helped her pick up the scattered pages of copy that had flown from her hand. After that, they stood looking at each other.

He stared at a tall, slim, sparklingly alive person with black hair in a flyaway tangle that stood out around her high-cheekboned face. Black lashes fringed the bluest eyes he had ever seen, but it was the smiling mouth that he couldn't seem to look away from. The upper lip was short, the lower one full and sensuous, and they were parted and tilted at the corners, showing small, perfect teeth.

Meeting the long stare from his deep-set brown eyes, Kelly felt a curious spark leap between them, although she knew instinctively they came from different worlds. Though she was a tall girl, she still had to tilt back her head to look at him. His crisp brown hair and calm face, uncompromising jawline, hard mouth, and expensive business suit told her he was a man of wealth and position.

She murmured the proper apologies and hurried through the heavy glass door of her office building. It was distinctly untypical of Jonathan Winslow Templeton the Third to pursue a chance meeting, but there he was when she paused to wait for the elevator. He asked her out and she accepted. He was Jack Templeton, from Boston, in Alaska on business. If, during that first evening, he told her what kind of business, it passed her by, for she was in a glorious state of enchantment. He amused her with his wit and clever conversation. He charmed her with bits of flattery, and surprised her with carefully chosen questions about herself. She found herself pouring out her life story and he listened, watching her expressive face, his eyes moving from her blue eyes to the unruly curls and often resting on her sweetly curved mouth.

When he walked her to the door of her apartment that first night, he kissed her. It was by no means Kelly's first kiss, but it shook her to her roots, and she trembled like a leaf. Jack, too, seemed shaken and Kelly remembered him looking down at her in a strange, almost angry way. When her eyes met his, her lips were trembling and he kissed her again, wildly, hungrily. Her arms went around his neck and desire flamed between them.

They spent every possible moment together and within a week Kelly went to bed with him and no words of common sense would have kept her from his arms. She had been out with men before, infatuated with some, half in love with others, but after that first evening with Jack, she was consumed by passion. When he made love to her she was incapable of thought, lost in a sensuous mist, totally responsive to his strong, slender hands and his hard, possessive lips. Jack made no secret of his desire for her, and after that first week, his need deepened into a naked hunger to which she reacted wildly.

After a session of wild lovemaking, he pro-
posed. He whispered hoarsely in her ear that he
had to have her—he wanted to marry her. Kelly
accepted without hesitation. He drew a deep
breath and pulled her against him and held her
fiercely, kissing her in a strange, tender, possessive way.

At the quiet wedding in City Hall, with one of
Jack's business associates and his wife as wit-
nesses, Kelly still felt that possessive attitude and
it thrilled her. Kelly had called Marty and Mike.
Marty had not been able to come on such short
notice and Mike said a flat "no" to the invitation,
but nothing mattered to Kelly as she waited for the
moment she and Jack would be alone.

When they returned to Kelly's apartment after
the wedding, there was a single yellow rose and a
card from Mike that read: "It makes no difference.
Love, Mike." Jack arched his brows when he read
the message, and asked who it was from. Kelly
found it difficult to explain her relationship with
Mike—though she tried. Later she realized that
marked the beginning of her husband's strange
possessiveness.

Jack took her to Boston. Kelly was awed by the
splendor of his home, the evidence of wealth and
position, and most of all by his sister, Katherine.
Two months later she knew she would never fit
into his life. She had fallen in love, immediately
and wildly. She had childishly married her Prince

Charming, without a single thought to the consequences, the repercussions, the kind of life she would be expected to live. Now, with little to do because they had a daily cleaning woman and a cook, Kelly wandered aimlessly around the apartment, like a bird in a gilded cage. Her husband flatly refused to allow her to get a job. She remained isolated in the apartment to await his homecomings.

Jack had become Jonathan. She could not think of him as Jack in their home. An abyss lay between them, bridged only at night, when he came to her in the darkened room. He merely had to lay down beside her and she could feel his pulse accelerate. She accepted his passion and returned it. She was most vulnerable at night and he simply had to kiss her and they would come together with a strange, hot need for each other that consumed Kelly. Afterward she would lie awake hour after hour, until finally, exhausted sleep claimed her. She awoke to reach out for him and find he was gone. What terror and what ecstasy the night held for her!

One day she came downstairs and heard Katherine and Jonathan—that's the way she thought of him now—in the den. Katherine had come to discuss the dinner party they were to give for an important business associate.

"Well, talk to her, Jonathan. If you don't approve of her behavior tell her so." The clear, assured voice came distinctly into the hall and Kelly paused beside the door.

"There are times when I think I shouldn't have married her," Jonathan said tiredly and then angrily slammed his hand down on the desk. "Damn, damn her!" he exploded.

"I knew the instant I set eyes on her that you had made a ghastly mistake," Katherine said drily.

"That's enough, Katherine!" His voice was bitter, harsh.

"Well, it's your problem. The sooner you get out of it the better."

"She's like a ghost wandering around here. I thought maybe if we had a child . . ."

"Heaven forbid! You would be out of your mind to consider having a child by that woman. She's unhappy because she is out of her element. She simply does *not* fit into a cultured world."

"I'm going out of my mind, anyway. I can't concentrate on this deal with Waterman Electronics. I don't know how she'll act this evening. She may move about like a robot, or hide in the kitchen. Something has got to give soon. I can't take much more of this."

"Don't worry about tonight. I've talked to the cook about the menu and ordered fresh flowers. I'll even send over a dress for her to wear. Don't worry, Jonathan. I'll take care of things. I always have."

"Thank you, Katherine. Will Nancy be here?"

"Of course. Nancy will keep the conversation flowing among the women. She will . . ."

Kelly walked stiffly down the hall and into the kitchen, where she leaned against the wall. What had she become? What kind of a fool was she to hover outside a door and listen to her husband discussing her so coldly? It seemed she had lost everything—pride, self-respect, husband.

"Coffee, Mrs. Templeton?" The cook was looking at her strangely. "It's in the dining room."

"Thank you," she murmured, but stood there for a moment before she was able to push herself away from the wall.

She met Jonathan and Katherine in the hallway. Katherine nodded coolly and went out the door. Jonathan stood inspecting her, his mouth compressed, a line etched between his dark brows. Almost guiltily she removed her fingers from the polished surface of the hall table. She had to fight the urge to lift the hem of her skirt and wipe away the offending prints.

"Why don't you go shopping today or get your hair done for tonight?"

"All right." Her voice was expressionless and she looked down at the fingerprints marring the polished wood.

"It's merely a suggestion, not an order," he snapped. "Most women would jump at the chance to have unlimited credit at the shops. You wander around this place like a ghost and dress to fit the part. Look at yourself. You wear things that make you melt into the woodwork." His lips held a slight sneer.

The pain that pierced her heart whitened her face. She looked away from him. Her gaze fell on the door at the top of the stairs, the sweet haven of her bedroom, and she longed to be there out from under the gaze of this stranger she had married. She hurt so much that it seemed a flood of tears was trapped inside her body, yet she could not cry. It was as if her pride had closed the valve on her emotions so tightly that there was no way to release them.

"For heaven's sake!" His harsh voice shattered the silence and he stared at her angrily, for a time saying nothing more.

Kelly couldn't bring herself to look at him. Finally she heard the click of his heels on the marble floor and the slam of the front door. She closed her eyes, wincing.

Somewhere along the way they had lost each other.

Kelly sincerely believed she had tried to find a place for herself among the wives of his friends. The cool reception she received on each overture of friendship was due, she was sure, to the influence of Katherine and Nancy. The men had seemed to enjoy her company, but after one informal party, when in desperation to keep from standing alone she had lingered among them to exchange bits of chitchat and laugh at their light flattery, she had felt Jonathan's piercing eyes from across the room, and Katherine's disapproval.

Cheap and vulgar flirting was the way Jonathan had put it that night when he lost his temper and lectured her with a cruel, icy tongue. He had marched her upstairs to their bedroom and made love to her as if she was a woman he'd paid for. After that, she realized, she had grown frightened of him and began shrinking from him, retreating farther and farther within herself in order not to risk his disapproval.

They had done each other great damage by getting married. She could never be anything except what she was. He could never take her lively, outgoing personality and reshape it to fit into his world. In the process of trying to do so he was destroying everything that was unique and alive about her that had attracted him to her in the first place. She had become quiet and withdrawn, a person she scarcely knew herself. If she had hurt Jonathan, she bitterly regretted it. She only knew he was not the man she had met in Anchorage and she could not continue living with him. There was only one thing to do.

Once she'd decided, Kelly's mind clicked into gear. While she packed, tears trickled down her face and ran into her mouth. She wiped her eyes and pushed damp fingers through her hair. Where had their love gone? It was dead! You couldn't

18

take warm, sweet love and put it in an atmosphere like this and expect it to survive. Divorce was easy these days. Jonathan would find a way to get it over with quickly—and without publicity. With her gone, the blame could be laid at her feet and he could save face.

She began to regain her self-respect. With it came anger like acid in her stomach. She thought about the reception she had received from his sister, about the cold, icy treatment her husband had given her, about the times he had spoken to her as if she tried to seduce every man she talked with. She remembered many times he had brought up Mike's name as if he were a stupid laborer with nothing on his mind but getting her to bed.

She had been the stupid one! She had no one to blame but herself, and it was up to her to get herself out of this impossible situation.

Kelly packed one large suitcase with the things she had brought with her, plus a few things Jonathan—when he was Jack—had bought for her in Anchorage. She placed the large sapphire and diamond ring on top of the note she left on the bedside table. On second thought, she placed her credit cards beside the note, which simply said that they both knew their marriage was a mistake and for him not to worry. She didn't want any kind of settlement—only her freedom. She regretted that she had been an embarrassment to him and to his sister.

19

Kelly walked out of the apartment building feeling like a new person. About the time Jonathan, Katherine, and Nancy were greeting their dinner guests, she was stepping off the plane in Portland, Oregon.

The trip had given Kelly time to organize her thoughts. On the way to the airport she had stopped at the bank and withdrawn the money her father had left her. She'd recounted it on the plane. Even after paying for her ticket, she had enough to tide her over until she could find a job.

She had learned advertisement layout at the newspaper in Anchorage. Her ads were good and original, and the salesmen who took them to the advertiser had little trouble selling them.

In Portland, Kelly found an efficiency apartment in a moderately priced building. After putting in a supply of food, she went to bed and stayed there for almost two days. She slept, got up and fixed herself a meal, then went back to sleep again. Not until she was in the quiet of her own place with no one to criticize her every move, did she realize how exhausted she was or how her nerves had stretched to almost the breaking point.

The first place she applied for a job hired her. The big, pleasant man who interviewed her was impressed with her knowledge of layout. There was one catch, however. She had to sell her own ideas to the advertisers. She would have a list of potential customers, no other salesman would infringe on her territory, and she would receive a commission, plus salary.

The first month she was astounded at the size of her commission check. She enjoyed her job, and being her own person once again. If she thought about Jack—she was back to thinking of him as Jack—he seemed a person she had met in a very nice dream. She never allowed herself to think about Boston. The months that had seemed so endless became blurred together in her head like a television show she had watched and half-forgotten.

Kelly had been in Portland for four months when she called Marty in Fairbanks and learned that Jonathan was looking for her. Marty giggled when Kelly told her about coming to Portland because that was the only connection she could make when her plane from Boston had reached Chicago. Marty explained that Mike had been especially worried about her after Jonathan, him-self, had come out to the resort looking for her. They promised to keep in touch and Kelly swore Marty to secrecy.

That Jonathan was looking for her didn't bother Kelly at all. Let him wait to get his divorce papers signed, she thought bitterly. The wait would pay him back, in some small way, for the miserable time she had spent with him.

The months turned into a year and Kelly began to get homesick for the cozy cabin deep in the

Alaskan bush. Soon the autumn snows would fall, and the clouds would scutter before the frigid winds. The days would become short, the nights long. Inside the cabin, warmed by a roaring wood fire, she would feel secure and at peace. She had saved more money than she had dreamed of saving in so short a time. Her little nest egg would go a long way toward putting the resort into operation again.

Kelly worked extra hard for another month, picked up her commission check, suffered through a farewell party given by fellow staff members, and caught a plane to Anchorage.

It was October. The Alaskan days were already short. Kelly sent word to Mike that she'd arrive on the afternoon train, and he was there waiting for her in the utility truck. He didn't ask any questions and she didn't offer any explanations.

The semi-darkened cabin was warm from the fire Mike had built in the fireplace before he came to meet her. He set her suitcases inside the door and went out to put the utility truck in the shed. She wished she didn't know how he felt about her. But it *was* good to be home and that thought crowded all others from her mind for the moment. She sighed heavily and sank down on the worn couch, pulled Aunt Mary's afghan over her, and went back to sleep.

CHAPTER TWO

EVERYTHING WAS AT peace in Kelly's world except her stomach, which was protesting loudly from lack of food. She dipped warm water from the reservoir and washed her face and hands. That would have to do for now. Tomorrow she would turn on the electric water heater and take a long, leisurely bath. As she stood there, Kelly's gaze was caught by her reflection in the small oak-framed mirror over the sink. At twenty-five she was hardly over the hill, yet she was disturbingly aware that she was no longer the young, starry-eyed creature who'd left the bush five years ago.

She still remembered what it was like those first few years. As she walked down the street, she positively beamed with the pleasure of living. People turned to stare at her not because she was so outstandingly beautiful, but because her face glowed with health and animation. Her walk, her whole being was suffused with robust enthusiasm that captured their attention.

Nothing brought a girl down to earth faster than a bad marriage, she thought, hanging up the towel. The sentimental dream-bubble of everlasting love with one man had burst, leaving her achingly empty.

The door opened and Mike's voice filled the cabin.

"Behold! Food cometh!" He kicked the door closed behind him and brought a small iron dutch oven to the cooking range. He lifted the lid and a delicious aroma wreathed up and filled the room.

"Chili! Smells great and I'm starved."

"Me, too. Get the bowls and we'll dig in." Mike hung his jacket on a peg beside the door.

"Not until I wash off two years growth of dust and mouse droppings." Kelly lifted the lid on the reservoir again and ladled hot water into a dish pan.

"A few mouse droppings won't hurt you." Mike grinned.

"Ugh! Don't talk about it!"

Kelly washed the bowls and the silverware, glancing occasionally at Mike's reflection in the mirror. He had turned a chair around and was straddling it. She could almost hear Aunt Mary say, "Michael, turn around and sit properly, for Pete's sake." Mike was looking older, too, Kelly thought, although they were both twenty-five. His hair was not quite as flaxen as it used to be, but it was still thick. He wasn't a handsome man; his face was too irregular for that. She could remember when she had been taller than Mike. Oh, how that used to bug him! Finally when they were about eighteen he had caught up with her, and now there wasn't a half-inch difference in their heights.

She felt guilty because she couldn't love him the

way he wanted to be loved. Sometimes she wished desperately that she could feel a soul-stirring pleasure in his arms, feel electrified by his touch. He was so comfortable, so dear. He deserved much more than she could give him.

"You're going to rub holes in those bowls," Mike said softly.

The silence was charged with expectancy. Their relationship from now on would depend on this evening. Oh, God! Kelly thought, she'd need help. She didn't want to hurt him.

"Maybe so, but they're clean. Fill them up and let's eat. My stomach thinks I've deserted it."

"That's not all you deserted," Mike said with his back to her. "Why in the hell did you marry him, Kelly?"

"Love. A vastly overrated emotion, as I soon discovered."

He set the bowls on the table and rested a hand on the top of her head. "I've missed you."

She nodded, not answering, not disputing. She had missed him too . . . and Marty. They had been a part of each other for most of their lives and her marriage had cut her off from them.

"What happened when Jonathan came here?"

Mike's wide mouth hardened. "Not much."

"But what?"

"He looked around the place like he was a king inspecting the hovels where the peasants live. I should have punched him in the nose." Mike got

25

up, opened a cabinet door, and slammed it shut. "I wish I'd brought some coffee."

"Go get it and I'll make a pot later," Kelly said absently.

Mike refilled his chili bowl. "What happened to the marriage?" he asked when he was sitting across from her again.

"I don't want to talk about it." Pain made her voice harsh.

"From what I saw of him, he's a stiff-necked, arrogant, smart-ass!"

"I don't want to talk about it, Mike. The marriage is over!"

"Not according to him. He said, and I quote, 'She is not getting a divorce. She will be my wife until the day she dies.'"

Kelly's eyes flicked up to meet his and she saw the anger there. Her face flushed under his probing stare.

She shrugged. "He'll get sick of that after a while. His sister will be on his tail to divorce me and eventually he will. In the meanwhile, I couldn't care less about what he does. I never intend to marry again, so he has more to lose than I do." She looked up to see what effect her words had on Mike, but his face was bent over his bowl and his spoon paused only momentarily on its way to his mouth.

He shot her a closed look. "How long are you going to stick around here?"

She laughed. "Trying to get rid of me already? Think I might interfere with your weekend orgies?"

He grinned, relaxing. "You've got to realize, woodenhead," he said, using his old pet name for her, "that I'm a man with all the normal urges and won't wait forever."

"I know, Mike. We're too much like brother and sister to ever be anything more. Remember, Mike, Mike, go fly a kite? And Kelly, Kelly, with a big, fat belly?"

"Yeah," he admitted. "It was fun growing up here. I wonder what would have happened to us if Uncle Henry hadn't taken us in."

"He never took you in, Mike. Aunt Mary worked hard and made the lodge pay off. My only regret is that she and Dad never married. I know they loved each other."

"Oh, I don't think they missed out on much," he said, with a satisfied smile. "I used to catch them kissing in the kitchen and every once in a while I'd see Uncle Henry pinch her on the bottom."

"You didn't! Why didn't you tell Marty and me?"

"Lots of things happened around here that I didn't tell you and Marty," he said insolently.

"That was stinking of you!"

"Yeah, wasn't it?"

"What other goodies didn't you tell us?" Kelly asked in an exasperated tone. This was a game

Mike played very well. In the old days he used to torment her and Marty with his "I know something you don't know" attitude and they would follow him for days trying to wheedle information out of him. "You haven't changed a bit!"

"You have," he leered, his eyes lingering on her soft, rounded breasts beneath the pullover knit shirt. He made a lecherous face. "Time has improved you! You used to be a skinny monstrosity with legs that came almost to your neck!"

"Well, thank you, vile creature! I can remember when your front teeth looked like Peter Rabbit's and your ears like Dumbo's, the elephant. I suppose, now that you've grown so handsome, you have to carry a stick to keep the girls away."

"Let's just say I don't miss any opportunities," he said wickedly.

It was easy for them to fall back into the light banter. It was as if they had never been apart. The only thing missing was Marty.

"Marty said she might come back if we open the resort," Kelly said suddenly, with a fierce longing to have the three of them together again.

"She mentioned it. I don't want to give up my job with the utility company just yet. It'll take a bit of money to put the old place back together again." Mike got up and reached for his coat. "Wash out the pot, woodenhead, and I'll fetch some coffee. Tomorrow I'll run you down to Talkeetna so you can stock up. That is if you're sure you're going to stay."

"I was never so sure of anything in my life. I don't think I ever want to leave this place again." She looked away, veiling her expression.

"Five years," he said softly. "You may be addicted to city life and don't know it."

"Go get the coffee, mister know-it-all. I'm a big girl, now, and I know my own mind, at last!"

"I hope so." He grinned. "It's taken you long enough." To emphasize the point, he slammed the door unnecessarily hard when he went out.

Kelly found the old blackened coffee pot, scrubbed it out, and filled it with water. She lifted a lid on the range and set the pot in the round hole so the flames lapped at its bottom.

It was good to be home. Although it was dark, she could see in her mind's eye the peaks of Mount McKinley dominating the skyline. Soon the snows would come . . . that breath of cold air Mike let in when he went out the door told her it could be any day now. The dark, drooping evergreens that shadowed the small settlement of three log cabins and a lodge seemed dreary and mysterious in the summer. But in the winter they appeared graceful and soft, skirted by snow.

There was a lot of work to be done, more than Kelly could possibly do alone, before the lodge would be ready to receive guests. The scrubbing alone would take ages. Another time-consuming chore would be cutting wood for the mammoth fireplace and for heat for her own cabin. That's about all she could depend on Mike doing. She had noticed the neat cords of wood beside his own cabin, probably not a winter's supply, but a good start. Maybe she could hire someone in Talkeetna to help.

Now that she was thinking about it, there were a million things to do and not much time to do them if they wanted to open when the season started. People liked a place to leave their snowmobiles before the highway got snowbound, because many of them would come up on the train, or by skiplane. They'd need a mountain of supplies, and a cook. A cook! That was one job she wouldn't do. She could cook up a meal for herself, but she couldn't on a large scale.

Ideas for advertising began to flick through her mind. They could place ads in the Anchorage and Fairbanks papers. There had been a big change in the economy ever since the oil companies had descended on the state. New corporations had sprung up and young executives had moved up from the States to run them. The country's huge size wouldn't stop them from taking a weekend in the bush. Skiplanes shuttled constantly back and forth between the resorts and the cities. Later, she mused, they could tap the vast resources of Seattle, Portland, and Vancouver for guests. For now, they would concentrate on getting them from closer to home.

Ever since the influx of "foreigners," as Alaskan natives called them, a powerful tide of newfound pride and racial identity had swept the state. Signs saying "Alaska For Alaskans," "Yankee Go Home," and "Happiness Is An Oklahoman Going Home With A Texan Under Each Arm," covered car bumpers. Kelly agreed to a certain extent. This was where she wanted to be, where she wanted to make something good and enduring; here, the only place in the world where she had roots, she didn't want the land spoiled with hamburger stands and neon lights.

Mike came in the door.

"Did you go all the way to Talkeetna to get that coffee?" Kelly teased.

"Had to see about my dogs." He handed her the coffee can and took off his coat.

"Dogs? You've got more than one?"

"I've got a sled team. They're half wild, so be careful."

"Are you going to race them at the Fur Rendezvous?"

"Not in the Anchorage to Nome race, but maybe in one of the shorter ones. I've only had them hitched together a few times. They're wilder than hell." He grinned.

"I want a dog. I can't remember a time when I didn't have one here."

"What kind do you want?"

"I don't care. Just a dog."

Mike went to the door, opened it, and yelled, "Charlie!"

A large, white, shaggy dog came bounding in with a frisbee in his mouth. He looked up at Mike expectantly and wagged his tail. Mike reached down and took the battered, chewed plastic disc. The tail stopped wagging and Charlie's eyes riveted to the frisbee.

"Not in the house, Charlie," Mike said sternly and the tail made a half wag. "Worthless piece of dog meat," he said affectionately and scratched the big head. "You got a two track mind. The frisbee and the . . . ball." Charlie jerked to attention on hearing the magic word. Mike laughed.

"Shame on you for teasing him," Kelly chided. "Come here, Charlie. What kind of a dog is he?"

"Part shepherd, part husky, I think. He's got to be part of something else with the disposition he's got. You can have him if you want him. He doesn't fit in with my sled team at all."

Charlie ambled over to Kelly and sniffed. She scratched his head and he leaned against her.

"How old is he?"

"Two years, I thought he'd outgrow playing with the frisbee and the ball, but it doesn't look like he's going to." Charlie peaked his ears on hearing the magic words again, and Kelly laughed, hugged his furry neck, and received a wet lick across her face for the trouble.

"Shall we team up, Charlie? I'll take care of you if you'll take care of me. What do you say?"

"I'll end up by taking care of both of you," Mike said drily. "Come on, Charlie, take this tooth punctured thing and get out of here." He held out the frisbee and Charlie clamped his teeth on it and bounded out the door. Mike shut it behind him.

Kelly washed mugs and filled them with coffee. "Is there an extra Citizen's Band radio around, Mike? We used to have one here and in the lodge."

"There's a good base station in the lodge. I'll fix it up and we'll run a couple of substations. Marty's talking about coming back and . . . she might want to open the other cabin."

"She wouldn't have to do that. She could move in here with me."

"I don't think she'd want to do that." Mike grinned knowingly.

"Well, are you going to tell me, or do I have to start wheedling?"

"Start wheedling."

"Oh, come on!"

"All right. If you're going to be that way about it, I'll tell you. It wouldn't surprise me if Marty brought a man back with her."

"Man? You mean she's going to get married?"

"You make it sound so . . . obscene."

"I didn't mean it that way. I'm surprised, that's

33

all. She didn't say anything about having anyone special."

Mike shrugged. "I don't know how special he is."

"Mike!"

He was watching her intently. "Don't get in a sweat. Marty's got a right to make her own mistakes."

"Then you don't like him?"

"Not especially, but that's not what's important, is it?" He got up and put on his coat. "I didn't like Jonathan Templeton, either." He was watching her, trying to read her face, and she looked up at him, her features torn by confused emotions.

"I can't imagine life without you and Marty." For the first time in months she felt weepy.

Mike's face had a strange, hard look on it, but it softened as he came toward her. He bent and kissed her cheek.

"See you in the morning. I've got the day off. We'll take a run up to Talkeetna and pick up a few things."

"I'm too tired to make out a list."

"Don't try. Bed down on the couch. Tomorrow we'll dig into the stuff up at the lodge and make this place livable."

"You're too good to me. What's the catch?"

"I've got designs on your body." He leered and his eyes raked her suggestively.

"Oh, get out of here, you . . . you . . . turkey! Now I know you're nuts!"

Kelly expected to fall asleep at once, but her mind refused to rest. Plans for the lodge, the comfortable relationship she had established with Mike, the prospect of Marty getting married, all blurred together in a swirl of thoughts. She tried to make her mind go blank but Jonathan's words sprang before her. "She will be my wife until the day she dies." Why would he say a thing like that unless he wanted to make Mike angry? But . . . Jonathan wasn't petty. He was probably frustrated because he couldn't get the divorce papers signed. She admitted, reluctantly, that *she* had been petty in making Katherine and Nancy wait for Jonathan's freedom. The marriage had, obviously, hurt him.

"I must divorce him," she said aloud, and the sound of her voice in the silent room startled her. She closed her eyes, feeling drained. Slowly sleep came to ease her troubled mind.

She woke once in the night with tears in her eyes and knew she'd been dreaming about Jack. Under the spell of her passion for him, the dreams they'd shared haunted her like an unforgotten melody. She could see his face, tender with love, bending to hers on their wedding night. "God, but you're beautiful, and you're mine. Say you love me. Say you love . . . only me." Jack faded away and Jonathan was shouting, "I never should have married her . . . damn her!" In the next breath, he muttered agonizingly, "Something's got to give. I can't take much more of this."

Kelly sank into an exhausted sleep and awoke only when she felt something rough and wet on her face. She opened one eye. Charlie was staring at her. She opened the other eye and saw the outside door open. Seconds later, Mike's square body filled it, and he kicked it shut after him. He brought in an armload of wood and knelt beside the fireplace.

"Are you going to lay on your butt all day? Get up, we've got things to do."

CHAPTER THREE

THE FIRST WEEK flew by. The second week ended and Kelly looked back with amazement at what she and Mike had accomplished. First, and most important, they had found Clyde and Bonnie Fisher, a middle-aged couple from Ardmore, Oklahoma. The Fishers had come to Alaska for better pay and found making a living just wasn't all that easy. But they loved the country and wanted to stay. Bonnie cooked fabulous, home-style meals, according to Clyde, and Clyde was about as handy as the pocket on a shirt, according to Bonnie. They both proved to be right.

"Think of the ads I can run in the papers! 'Come to Mountain View Lodge and meet Bonnie and

Clyde.'" From the very first Kelly felt as if she had known them forever.

"That's the only reason I married that ugly ol' boy," Bonnie said with spirit, her twinkling eyes seeking out Clyde. "I looked all over the country for a man named Clyde. I swore I was goin' to get me one. We was goin' to be Bonnie and Clyde. Well, this ugly ol' cowboy was the only thing I could find, so I took 'im."

"And I let 'er catch me 'cause she's fat and soft and keeps me warm on cold nights."

They were a perfectly matched couple and Kelly loved the good-natured banter that passed between them. They would live in the lodge in the room behind the kitchen, and be more or less responsible for it. Salary didn't matter too much, as long as they had a place to live and food to eat.

The first snow began falling one night and by morning it was a foot deep. Kelly looked out the window at the strange, haunting beauty of a monochromatic landscape, set against the deep blue of the winter sky. She put the copper teakettle on the cookstove and went back to the window to watch Charlie dig his nose deep in the snow and come up with his battered frisbee. He came to the window and stood looking at her, tail wagging. Kelly couldn't resist his silent plea.

The instant she opened the door he was there, frisky and playful. Shivering in the cold, she took the frisbee and sailed it far out into the air. Charlie bounded after it, leaped, and caught it in his mouth. He stood looking at the closed door, then with a toss of his head, he threw his toy up in the air, then pounced on it when it landed.

Kelly continued to play with Charlie on her way to the lodge. "You're just an overgrown pup, Charlie!" Kelly had put on her old red down-filled jacket and her yellow wool toboggan cap. Her makeup-free face was sparklingly alive. "I've more important things to do than play. One of these days you're going to work, too. I'm going to hitch you up to my old sled. But not today . . . so have fun while you can."

Kelly left her boots on the mat inside the door of the lodge and let her gaze wander around the cozy room. A fire was roaring in the massive stone fireplace that held an eight-foot log. The room was not large, but uncurtained, double-paned windows gave it an appearance of spaciousness. The "family room," as they called it, shone with new pride. Even the potbellied stove at the far end of the room had a new coat of stove blacking to cover the few rust spots the idle years had given it. In this cold climate heating was a main concern and each of the three private bedrooms, as well as the dormitory room that held eight bunk beds, had wood-burning stoves. Guests would eat their meals at the long trestle tables set up in the cozy lodge kitchen. In the bush they didn't expect all the modern conveniences.

Comfortable couches against the walls sported bright new slipcovers that matched the indoor-outdoor carpeting put down for extra warmth, and soft bearskin rugs added a native touch. Several beautiful fur pelts were stretched and nailed to the walls, as were Kelly's father's collection of primitive Alaskan tools. Sets of fur-lined chairs stood adjacent to the windows so guests could enjoy the view of Mount McKinley on clear days.

Kelly was excited to see that everything was ready to receive the guests who would be arriving the next day. Two couples were coming up on the train from Anchorage and Clyde would meet them in the four-wheel drive carry-all. Mike was on emergency-call for the utility company and had to remain near the Citizen's Band radio.

Marty was coming home to stay at the end of the week. She had made one quick trip to the resort before resigning from her job in Fairbanks and had brought her fiancé with her. Kelly had decided she liked him even if Mike didn't. She suspected Mike secretly thought no man was good enough for his twin.

Marty had introduced her fiancé as Trampel P. Thornburg, and Kelly had thought, good grief why would anyone name a child Trampel? But Marty called him Tram, which wasn't so bad. He was a ski instructor and a wildlife photographer. He and Marty would occupy the third cabin and together they would arrange cross-country ski tours or overnight camping expeditions for the extra hardy wildlife enthusiasts. Many tourists loved winter safaris, especially those that offered excellent opportunities to observe caribou, moose, and wolf.

"Are you goin' to stand there admirin' or are you comin' to eat these flapjacks?" Bonnie called from the kitchen door.

"Flapjacks, again? I'll be so fat I won't be able to reach the table!"

"Well, land sakes! You're so skinny a good Oklahoma norther would blow you clear down to Texas. Get yourself on in here, now. You need somethin' that'll stick to your backbone with all the work you've been doin'."

Bonnie's square body was bundled up in a bright blue jogging suit complete with turtleneck sweater topped with a bibbed apron. She waddled around in fur-lined moccasins.

"Bonnie! What are you going to wear when it really gets cold?" Kelly's eyes had a vivid sparkle. "All you need is earmuffs and you'll be ready to trek to the top of the mountain!"

"If there's anything this Oklahoma girl hates more than Texas football, it's cold! I'm here to tell you I'm not pokin' my head out of this here lodge till spring!"

"You're priceless! Where's Clyde?"

"He's out on the end of that chain saw again. Give that man anything with a motor and movin' parts and he's as happy as if he had good sense."

In the late afternoon Kelly stuck her head out the door of her own cabin and called to invite Mike in for coffee. Closing the door, she viewed the room proudly. She loved the cozy, neat home she had shared with her father during her growing-up years. She remembered the winter they made the braided rug that covered the floor. He had braided the wool strips and she had sewn them together with nylon fishing line. It was as bright and as durable now as when new. A pillow-lined couch with a freshly washed slipcover stood on one side of the fireplace and a rocking chair on the other. A floor-to-ceiling bookcase which also housed the stereo set she had sent down from Anchorage when she gave up her apartment, and a winter's supply of reading material, helped to turn the cabin into a home. Although not fancy by city standards, it gave Kelly a feeling of permanence and security.

She set two mugs and a plate of Bonnie's freshly baked chocolate chip cookies on the trestle table that divided the kitchen from the rest of the room and smiled at Mike when he came in. He pulled off his boots and hung his coat on a peg.

"Sit down and ruin your appetite for supper." Kelly lifted the graniteware coffee pot from the stove.

"It would take more than what you're offering to do that," Mike said, reaching for a cookie. "Now if I could find me a woman who could cook like Bonnie, I might even marry her."

Kelly poured the coffee, then paused to listen before she returned the pot to the stove. "Do you hear a chopper?"

"Yeah, guess I do. The rangers up in the park have one, but they seldom come down this far."

The sound of the helicopter came closer and Kelly went to the window to peer out.

"You don't suppose our guests decided to fly in tonight instead of taking the train tomorrow?" she asked with a worried frown.

"So what? We'll get one more night's lodging out of them. Sit down and drink your coffee. Clyde's already on his way out to meet the helicopter. I can hear him grinding on the starter."

Kelly turned on another lamp and sat down across from Mike. Soon they heard the helicopter take off again and then the sound of a car returning from the clearing where it had landed.

"I should go up to the lodge and meet the guests."

"Let Bonnie handle it," Mike said reaching for another cookie. "She's already got enough stuff baked to feed an army."

Kelly laughed. "If I don't knock off eating so much, I'll have to spend my vacations at a fat farm."

"You look a sight better than when you first came home. You looked like a starved alley cat."

Mike's strong mouth deepened into a genuine grin.

"That's what I like about you. You say such nice things."

The car stopped in front of the cabin. Kelly saw the lights shining on the snow through the window. Then a car door slammed shut and someone hammered on the door.

"Who was the wise guy who said Bonnie could handle it?" she said as she got up.

She flung open the door and a man's frame filled the doorway, his bare, snow-dusted head almost touching the top. Jonathan! He was wearing a sheepskin coat and carried a large suitcase in each hand. The chill that struck Kelly had nothing to do with the wind coming in.

Jonathan's dark eyes took in every detail of her appearance—her worn jeans and a faded flannel shirt that revealed her white throat and the tops of her unencumbered breasts. His bitter stare made the color rise to flood her face, all except her white lips, which parted and whispered a silent "No!"

His face was harsh and powerful, the jaw jutted in angry determination, the mouth straight and very hard. Kelly looked around, as if for someplace to go. In her dazed state, she realized Mike was on his feet. She turned slowly to meet piercing brown eyes. At once her mind jerked awake.

"What are you doing here?"

Mike moved up beside her and Jonathan stood silently, dwarfing them, his broad shoulders tense. He moved into the room and dropped his suitcases. Kelly closed the door and stood with her back to it.

"I asked what you're doing here!" Her voice echoed shrilly. She drew in her lower lip, her face stiff with brittle cynicism.

"I came to see my wife. What do you think?" His mouth twisted caustically.

Her body tensed as she tried to stop trembling. Her blue eyes flickered restlessly, not touching on her husband, whose presence seemed to fill every corner of her mind. Damn it! Here she was quaking like a timid rabbit, just as she had done in Boston.

"I don't want you here!" Her voice had savage, raw feeling in it. "I'll sign your papers. You can stay at the lodge tonight, but I want you out of here in the morning."

Jonathan's features hardened even more. He glanced at Mike, who was watching him with a taut expression.

"I'm staying and the sooner you realize it the better." The icy eyes dared Mike to interfere.

"If Kelly doesn't want you here," Mike said through tight lips, "you're going, and that's all there is to it."

Jonathan hit him. One moment the two men

were glaring at each other and the next Mike was flying across the room and landing with a thud against the trestle table. It was over before Kelly could intervene.

She ran over to him. "Mike? Mike? Are you hurt?"

He sat up, rubbing the back of his head. "What do you think? I don't bang my head on the table everyday."

Kelly stood up and turned on Jonathan. "What's gotten into you? You had no reason to hit Mike," she said furiously.

Jonathan's hard-boned face was taut with rage. His hands clenched and unclenched. He looked as if he wanted to strangle the two of them.

"No reason? You better get him out of here or I'll kill him."

For a moment Kelly was lost for words. In the eight months she had lived with this man, he had never shown this kind of violence.

"You'd better go, Mike. I'll talk to him," she said quietly, her eyes begging him to obey.

"You're sure?" He darted a look of pure hatred at the man standing in a pool of water that dripped from his snow-covered boots.

"Yes, I'm sure." She reached behind Jonathan and plucked Mike's coat from the peg. Mike shrugged into it and put his stocking feet into his boots. As if to assert his authority over the situation, Jonathan stepped over, opened the door, and slammed it shut after Mike passed through. Immediately, he turned on Kelly and the look of fury on his face made her shake with a totally new fear.

"You adulterous witch!"

In the months before she'd left him she had seen him angry, but nothing like this. During the more than a year since they had seen each other, he had changed, aged, grown more bitter. Now, anger raged between them like a forest fire, scorching everything in its path. He jerked off his coat and hung it up, his powerful body tense with suppressed emotion.

"I could kill you for what you've done to me," he said when he turned to face her.

Silence stretched between them like a taut rubber band. Kelly walked on unsure legs to the cookstove and picked up the graniteware pot. Automatically she took a clean mug from the hook and poured coffee into it as well as into her own.

"How did you know I was here?"

"I've known every move you've made since a month before you left Portland." He sat down at the table.

The smell of the coffee made Kelly feel sick but she sipped it anyway. "It's nice to know I've been spied on," she said coolly.

"It took a while, but I found you," he said without looking at her.

"What took you so long? I've been here almost three weeks."

He drew in a harsh breath and moved restlessly, his dark eyes probing hers. "I had plans to make. Company responsibilities to delegate to others."

Kelly looked up, startled. She had no idea what to say to him. She looked down at his hands cradling his cup. They were pale and cold.

"Say something," he ordered. "Why do you think I left my business, Boston, my family and friends? Because . . . if you can't live in my world, I'll live in yours!"

Kelly stared at him without understanding, her lashes flickering up and down over her blue eyes. "You're not staying here! I don't want you here!" she blurted out.

He set his cup down and reached across the table to grab her wrist. "Why did you walk out on me without a word?" Kelly tried to pull her wrist free, but his fingers tightened. "Answer me!" he roared.

"I left you a note. It was more than you deserved."

"Katherine found your rings and credit cards in your room just before I was expecting an important guest. Why did you do it?" She could feel the tremor in the fingers that gripped her wrist.

"I explained in the note."

"Note? What note? I haven't heard one word from you in fourteen months and two days! Don't you think you owed it to me to tell me you were leaving?"

Kelly's temper flared. "I said I left you a note! Your sister, the keeper of the family's snobbish honor, probably snatched it to keep it from contaminating her precious brother. Don't you dare call me a liar, Jonathan Winslow Templeton the Third!" she said with a sneer. "I've got the starch back in my backbone and I'll never cower under anyone's glare again!"

Jonathan drew in a deep breath. "I never intended to make you cower. I hated it when you moved around the house like a ghost. Why didn't you talk to me, tell me what was wrong?"

Kelly looked up at him in disbelief. They hadn't talked during those last few months they'd lived together. They had spoken the same language, but they'd never communicated, except in bed. He wouldn't have understood how she felt, wouldn't understand now. She'd been his toy, a possession to set in the corner and take out and play with when the mood struck. From the day she walked into that luxurious nightmare she had not been allowed to be herself, only a shell of what the Templetons wanted her to be. Well, thank God, she'd gotten out of it. She would never go back!

"You could have called and told me where you were," he insisted after a moment, releasing her arm.

"There was nothing to say. I didn't need you. I can take care of myself."

"Nothing to say?" He leaned toward her, suppressed rage expressed in the flare of his nostrils and the tightness of his mouth. "You're my wife!"

"You should have thought of that before you allowed your sister to relegate me to the position of live-in whore."

"What do you mean by that?"

"I was never your wife. I never measured up to the Templetons," Kelly flared. "Why did you marry me?" she demanded.

Silence fell between them while his eyes moved from her face to the open neck of her shirt and down over the curves of her breasts. He bent over the table and stared deliberately before bringing his eyes up to hers.

"I think you know why." His voice was slurred, charged with emotion. "Don't tell me you didn't enjoy our sex life, because I know you did."

"So that's why!" She shuddered and looked away. "Sex! You should have propositioned me. You might have gotten what you wanted without marrying me."

"Shut up! I won't stand for that kind of talk from you." His head jerked up in pain and rage and his dark eyes blazed with anger.

"You won't stand for . . ." Kelly choked on her anger. "The biggest mistake of my life was marrying you, Jonathan Winslow Templeton the Third!"

"Damn it! Stop calling me that!" he thundered and banged his fist down on the table.

Kelly bit back her intended reply and fought down the impulse to slap him. Not trusting herself to sit opposite him, she got up and went to lean against the fireplace mantel. Absently she opened the door of the clock case and started the pendulum of the clock swinging.

Jonathan sat at the end of the table and surveyed the room. It was impossible to tell what he was thinking as he regarded the worn couch, the blue and black cookstove, the metal, mail-order kitchen cabinets.

"Why did you stop calling me Jack?" He asked the question quietly. For a fleeting moment Kelly thought she heard pain in his voice, but she dismissed the thought.

"You were no longer Jack when we got to Boston," she said flatly.

"What do you mean? I was the same person."

"You were not!" Anger and resentment flared again.

"I'm tired of arguing," he said. "I'm hungry. What's there to eat?"

"You can eat at the lodge where you'll sleep," she snapped.

Jonathan's answer was to take off his boots. For the first time he seemed to notice the water created by the melted snow he had tracked in. He set the boots against the wall, beneath his coat, and went to the cabinet to unroll a length of paper toweling. He squatted down, blotted away the puddles, and threw the damp toweling into the fire.

Kelly gazed into the blaze, her head resting on her arm on the mantel. His arm went about her waist and he pulled her back against him. She stood rigid as she felt his hot lips against the cool skin on the back of her neck. The swift, panic-beat of her heart echoed the deep thud of his.

"Go away!" The gasping sound came from her as if she were suffocating. "I don't want you!" She waited tensely for him to release her.

She cried out in pain as he took hold of the hair at the back of her head and jerked her around to face him. She tried to move her head in protest, but couldn't avoid the lips that swooped down on hers. His kiss was an outright act of possession, a blistering insult. He ground her mouth beneath his own in reckless disregard, his teeth crushing her lips. She wanted to fight him off, hit him with her fists, scratch him with her nails, but some instinct warned her that to react in such a way would only arouse his temper more. Instead she kept perfectly still, her lips compressed. Slowly his lips softened. When she didn't respond, he lifted his head.

"Open your mouth!" he said harshly, his eyes blazing with anger. She froze, recoiling from his violence.

She was so close she could see the changes the last year had made in his face. There was an extra leanness in the planes of his cheeks, and new lines about his eyes. The bitterness reflected there struck her so forcibly that she flinched.

"Is he a good lover?" he said through clenched teeth. "Does he satisfy you?" His hands moved to her shoulders and gripped them tightly.

Incredulous, she stared at him, "You . . . ! Mike isn't my lover!"

"I'm not a fool. I saw the way he looked at you!" His face contorted savagely, his jaw held in a vice. "Do you think I've forgotton the note he sent you on our wedding day, or the number of times you've mentioned his name?" He was shaking her shoulders, his fingers hurting.

Kelly stared at him, eyes wide in her flushed face. "I hardly mentioned him or Marty to you after . . . those first few weeks."

"I should have counted the number of times I heard you say . . . Mike did this . . . or that. We did this . . . or that, meaning you and him! You even talked about this place in your sleep."

She was taken aback, and lowered her lashes, trying to think. "What if I did? This is my home. Look around, Jonathan. It may not have marble floors and crystal chandeliers, but its home and it's mine!"

"Ours!" he corrected.

"Mine!" she said stubbornly, "and I don't want you here."

"Ours!" he said again.

"Go away!" she hissed and tried to jerk away, but he held her immobile. "You've no right to come here."

His lips curled back from his straight white teeth in a hard sneer. "That's where you're wrong. I have three rights. One, my wife is here and I'm going to live with her. Two, when we were married you signed your portion of this property over to me to handle for you. And three . . . I have paid six years of back taxes on this property and that gives me the right to live here. It also gives me the right to say who will live here with me!"

"I don't believe you!" she gasped. "You wouldn't . . ."

"It depends on you, little wife. It depends on you."

CHAPTER FOUR

FOR A MOMENT Kelly couldn't move. She felt his eyes probe fiercely all the way down to her legs that were suddenly cold and shaking, although her face burned as though with a fever. He released her shoulders and she turned and walked slowly into her bedroom, closing the door behind her.

She stared at the stranger looking back at her from the mirror over her dressing table. She stood there for a moment, trembling, accepting that Jonathan was here and that he intended to stay. He was the Jonathan of Boston dressed differently.

"Oh, help," she muttered and looked away from the pale face and vacant eyes. What did he mean about her signing the property over to him? She had signed papers so he could handle the probate of her father's will, the clearing of the title, and the paying of the inheritance tax. Could he force Mike and Marty from the only home they had ever known? He couldn't! The three of them had put all the money they could scrape together into fixing up this place. By working hard, they could make a living here. "No!" she said aloud and wished she had the courage to pick up the chair and smash something! What was she going to do? They'd worked so hard! Tears sprang into her eyes and she blinked them away. She felt so . . . betrayed!

She was standing in the middle of the room, seeing nothing, her mind whirling in an eddy of bewilderment, when the door opened behind her.

"No," she said hoarsely before she turned to face him. "No," she said again. Her blue eyes were strained and over-bright. "You're not staying here, Jonathan. Go up to the lodge. One of us will be leaving in the morning."

He came into the room carrying the two heavy suitcases and stood looking around. The door to the small bathroom was open and he headed for it. He had to angle the bags through the narrow door to reach the other bedroom.

Kelly followed him through the bathroom and stood in the doorway. "You don't take *no* for an answer, do you, Jonathan? I said I don't want you here."

"I don't think you've given this much thought, Kelly. I didn't want to tell you I have the controlling interest here. I was perfectly willing to let things stand as they were, but you forced me to use that lever. Now you can either tell your friends that they have thirty days to clear out of here, and I'll give them that long, or you can face the fact that I'm here to live with you as your husband and make the best of the situation."

"You're inhuman! You don't care about anything except what you want. You think you can come here and order me to accept you in my home and make you welcome. I was never made to feel welcome in *your* home! Do you have any idea how I felt after the first few weeks? Like a nonentity, an invisible person."

His dark brows drew a heavy line over his eyes. "There was no reason for you to feel that way. I gave you everything I could think of that—"

"Gave! Gave! You gave me everything except yourself, your time!" she shouted.

"You're hysterical. You didn't like my way of life and made no effort to fit into it. I'm here to show you that I can fit into your way of life."

"Then what?"

"Then we'll pick up where we left off."

"You're out of your mind! I'll never go back there! Never! You're not a human being. You're a computer, programmed to give orders and take what you want without regard to ordinary people like me and Marty and Mike. You've no feelings as simple as love, fear, longing for something, working for it. Everything you have has been served up to you on a silver platter. What do you know about people like me?" She clung to the door frame, rage making her weak. "You don't understand me. You never understood why I married you!"

"I understood a lot more than you realize." Jonathan's eyes had not left her face. "I understand you were unhappy in Boston and you're happy here. I understand that's why you left me, and not because you didn't love me."

"You've got to be the most conceited man alive!" She laughed in hollow irony. "You don't love a man who hides you away and takes you out occasionally, and watches you like a hawk to see you don't disgrace him. You don't love a man who barks at you and keeps you running to do his bidding like a nervous dog. Most of all, you don't love a man who keeps you in his home where the only communication you have is in the night . . . in the dark . . . when he isn't reminded that you're a simple girl with red blood . . . and not . . . blue!"

During this outpouring of harsh words Jonathan stood quietly. Only his eyes moved, becoming bright with inner rage. His face remained shuttered.

"Why didn't you tell me this before?" She could tell he was angry, but his voice remained calm.

"So you could discuss what was to be done about me with your sister? So you could take all my feelings out and hold them up for ridicule? Give me credit for a little more brains than that."

"Now you're being stupid," he said without looking at her. He lifted one of his suitcases up onto the bed, opened it, and began laying out stacks of socks and underwear. "Couldn't you have let me know you were safe?" He turned abruptly to look at her. "Do you have any idea of the anguish you put me through when you just disappeared? I had detectives searching everywhere I could think of."

"How did you find me?"

"I resorted to bribery. I corrupted an employee of the Social Security Department and, when your employer paid your tax into the treasury, I got his name."

"That's against the law!"

"I didn't give it a thought." He was staring at her pale, subdued profile. "You look older."

"I am older. A hundred years older."

"And you're different."

"After what I've been through, how could I possibly remain the same?" she flung at him bitterly.

Rage flashed in his eyes, darkened his face, and hardened the lines of his mouth. He moved so fast she had no time to slip back through the doorway. His hands gripped her shoulders.

"Do you think you're the only one who suffered? You've driven me crazy, wondering where you were, who you were with, and what was happening to you."

She tried to strike his hands away. "Don't touch me."

"I don't care what you want! I want to touch you. I want to feel every inch of you against me and I will! Do you understand, Kelly? We're man and wife for as long as we live. The only thing that will change that fact is . . . death! And I'm mighty tempted to kill you for what you've put me through."

She believed him and was terrified, but determined not to show it. "Have you worked out your method, or just dreamed about it?"

"When I get my hands on you, murder is the last thing I'm thinking of," he said harshly and crushed her to him.

She pushed at his chest as he drew her closer. "Let me go! I said I don't want you to touch me. I hate it!"

"Then you'll learn to love it again, because I'll touch you when and where I want to!"

Instinctively, she felt he was about to lose control, but desperately and recklessly she goaded him. Words fell out of her in a torrent, blatant lies, out of place, wrong, jarring.

"Mike is my lover! I want him, not you. I'm divorcing you and going to him. I'm crazy about him and I sleep with him every night and I'll sleep with him tonight and tomorrow night. Find yourself another woman, Jonathan. I don't want you!"

"Damn you!" he muttered. His hands encircled her upper arms and her eyes darkened as they hardened into bands. His face was like carved granite, hard and bitter. Kelly closed her eyes, sure he was going to hit her. Instead his hands slipped up around her neck and closed about her throat. She gasped, trying to pull away, but his mouth came down on hers, savagely, relentlessly, prying her lips apart, grinding his teeth against her mouth. The thumbs beneath her chin and the fingers behind her head kept her immobile beneath his consuming mouth. She moaned at the pain he was inflicting on her and struggled so violently that their bodies swayed and crashed against the wall.

He moved too fast for her. He dragged her to the bed, pushed her down, and fell on her. Winded, they lay there, breathing hard. His dark head shut out the overhead light and his mouth burned, delved, bruised her own, forcing her to surrender her lips. His hands moved possessively over her. During the struggle, her shirt had become unbuttoned and his fingers slid inside to find the high, warm swell of her breast.

He raised his head and stared at the white skin laid bare by the open shirt. His fingers loosened and moved slowly, gently, in a caressing motion.

The smooth, warm fingers softly caressed her trembling body. Her heart beat so hard she was deaf. She couldn't think. She couldn't speak.

Jonathan's eyes flickered to her face and she shook her head in silent protest. She couldn't bear the thought of submitting to him with this terrible chasm between them.

"Let me have you, darling," he whispered, and she heard the words through the singing of her blood and couldn't answer. Desperately she fought down the desire that spiralled crazily inside her.

"To hold you, touch you like this drives me crazy," he said in a strange, thickened voice, his mouth at her throat, then sliding up to close over her mouth, gently now. Her mouth quivered weakly under the persuasion of his kiss. The searching movement parted her lips and he began sensuously exploring the inside of her mouth with his tongue.

A strange, melting heat began inside her. The hungry, coaxing movements of his mouth were awakening the first, tentative response in her. One of his hands slid back and forth across her breast in a soft, possessive caress and her nipple, loving the feel of his palm, reacted automatically. Oh, the weight of him felt so good! She had missed the way he made her feel, the way he could force her to relinquish control, and fly away with him into the sensuous world where there were only his lips, his hands, the hard strength of his male body. Her lips began moving under his, clinging, returning the pressure of his mouth. She wanted him. She ached with the slow burning fire he was awakening in her body.

"I mean to have you," he groaned into her mouth and his body moved on hers urgently.

Abruptly, as though he had lifted her out of the well of sexual chaos, she went cold and stiff. "No," she said tightly. "No!"

"Oh, Kelly!" His voice was like a sound from the past, but she refused to be softened by the memory of the husky cry wrung from him at the peak of overwhelming pleasure.

She twisted out from under him and he let her go. He lay where she left him, breathing hard. At the door she turned back. He was sitting on the edge of the bed watching her.

"We were never suited. This was all we ever shared. It isn't enough. We must face it. Our marriage was a mistake." She saw him flinch as though she had struck him. "I didn't fit into your life and you won't fit into mine. It's best you forget I ever existed."

As she turned away, he said quickly, "I haven't totally disrupted my life to be put off so easily, Kelly. I'm staying. Forever, if necessary."

"I can't believe you want me when I despise everything you are, everything you stand for!" she cried.

His dark eyes mocked her. "What a liar you've turned out to be, Kelly," he drawled. "That isn't true and you know it. You can say all the words you want about hating me, but we both know differently, don't we?"

She wanted to slap him so badly her palm burnt. Self-respect made her resist with all her willpower and she clamped her lips down on the denial that bubbled up within her. She walked in silence through the bathroom, into her own darkened bedroom, and to the front door, where she began to jerk on her boots.

"You're not leaving here, Kelly." Jonathan stood in the doorway of her father's room.

"I'm going to the lodge and you can't stop me."

"Yes, I can stop you," he said calmly, "but don't force me. Get on that radio and ask Clyde to bring us something to eat. I haven't had a thing all day."

"I won't treat Clyde like a busboy! He isn't paid to bring me my meals," she replied coolly.

"He won't mind doing it this once. After this we'll either go to the lodge for our meals or you can fix them here. Tonight we're going to be here, alone. You can get on that radio or I will, and you know how snobbish a Bostonian can be when demanding service." He waited for her to speak. "Clyde will understand. I told him I was your husband and we'd been apart for a while, but that we're back together again."

Kelly felt suddenly sick, filled with humiliation and self-contempt for what happened in the bedroom. "Stay away from me," she snapped as he moved toward her. The burning temptation to give in to him was too new. The inevitability of her own submission was not the worst thing preying on her mind. It was the shameful truth that Jack wouldn't need to force her. He could take her whenever he chose. Already she was thinking of him as Jack again. There was nowhere to run. She was imprisoned, with snow and ice all around her and no choice but to submit to whatever he demanded. Of course she could defy him, but could she do that to Marty and Mike? There wasn't the slightest doubt in her mind that he would carry out his threat to put them out of their home. Maybe if she played along until she could see a lawyer in Anchorage . . .

Jonathan watched her closely, his own face expressionless. Kelly felt a shiver run down her spine.

"Don't . . . do this to me, Jonathan." The soft plea was out before she could bite it back.

"Poor Kelly. What a predicament!"

His mockery stiffened her spine. "I'm glad you think it's so funny!" She glared at him, her eyes alive with angry tears. "It's a game with you. You don't care who you hurt."

"I care, Kelly," he insisted flatly. "I'm fighting for what I want the only way I know how."

Kelly took off her boots. Her head ached and her dry throat hurt when she swallowed. She sat down beside the Citizen's Band radio and pressed the key on the desk microphone.

"Break . . . Mountain View base station. Are you on the channel, Bonnie?" Jonathan stood watching her and she gave him a withering look.

"Yes-sir-ee, I'm here. Ain't ya comin' up to eat, Kelly?"

Kelly closed her eyes and gritted her teeth before pressing the key to answer. "Not tonight, Bonnie. I was wondering if Clyde would mind bringing something down for us."

"Course he will, honey. Land sakes, I don't blame you none for wanting to be alone with that husband of yours. Why, you just stay right there and I'll send Clyde down with a dish of that chicken casserole you like and a fresh-baked blueberry pie. You got coffee, ain't ya?"

"Yes, I have coffee."

"Ten-four, Kelly. Say, honey, ya got the cookstove going, don't ya?"

"Ten-four."

"You might have to heat the casserole up a bit. Mike ain't been up for supper. Is he down there?"

"Negative. Mike, if you're on the channel, let Bonnie know if you're going up for supper."

There was a pause, then Mike's voice came in. "I'll be coming up in a few minutes, Bonnie. You okay, Kelly?"

"Sure. See you tomorrow. Thanks, Bonnie. Tell Clyde this won't be a regular thing."

"You get the coffee goin' and I'll send down everything but the candles and champagne. I'll be clear with ya, honey. You all enjoy yourself, now."

When Kelly looked at the doorway where Jonathan had stood, it was empty. She sat for a moment and tried to calm down. If he had been standing there with a mocking, "I told you so" look on his face, she might have hit him. She ran her tongue around the velvety innerside of her lips, which were still sore from his brutal kisses. Defiance and consternation swept through her, and she thought again what a naive idiot she had been to actually believe a man like Jonathan Winslow Templeton could love a girl like her. He was just frustrated now because she had left him. A man like Jonathan couldn't accept rejection.

The dryness in her throat reminded her of the bottle of Scotch in the cupboard. On her way to get it, she looked at herself in the mirror over the kitchen sink. You're a romantic, Kelly, she thought. She stared into serious eyes, dark circled and bright from tears she was too stubborn to shed. She'd read too many novels where the poor girl married her prince and they lived happily ever after. It was not a romantic world anymore and marriage was not a singular state. It was more of a stage in people's lives, different partners for different periods. Few stayed married forever and no one lived happily ever after.

She took the bottle from the cupboard, poured herself a stiff drink, and drank it in one gulp. She gasped. The fiery liquid burned all the way to her stomach. She leaned against the cabinet and coughed, tears blurring her eyes. Through her misery she felt a hand on her back and jerked away.

"Take your hands off me!" She struggled, flailing her arms.

"How much of that did you drink?"

"None of your business," she snapped, and pushed away from him. She opened the front of the firebox on the cookrange, uncaring that ashes drifted to the floor, and poked several small pieces of firewood into the opening before kicking it shut. Holding the coffee pot in front of her like a shield, she went to the sink. Jonathan stepped out of her way and she dumped the used grounds and refilled the pot with water. She heard the motor of the pickup as it approached the cabin, then the sound of the car door banging shut.

Jonathan held the door open for Clyde, who had a large covered tray in his hands. He stood just inside the doorway.

"I ain't supposed to track snow all over your clean floor," he said and grinned. "Bonnie done gave me strict orders."

"I'll take it then, Clyde. Don't want you to get

into trouble with the wife." Jonathan took the tray. "Don't run off, though. Kelly and I were just having a drink and would like you to join us. Wouldn't we, darling?"

Kelly turned her back to him and forced a civil reply. "Of course."

"No, don't bother, Mr. Templeton. Bonnie told me to shake a leg on back."

"Jack. My name's Jack," Jonathan said easily. "I'm afraid all we've got is water to go in the Scotch unless you'd rather have a straight shot."

"Straight will be fine."

Jonathan searched the cupboard and brought out a small wine glass. He poured from the bottle and carried the drink to Clyde still standing on the mat beside the door.

"I hear you're from Oklahoma, my favorite state. I spent a year at Tinker Airforce Base in Oklahoma City and got addicted to the place. How do the Cowboys look this year? Think they've got a chance to stomp O.U. again?"

"They got a damn good chance. They got a running fullback from a little town called Bowlegs, Oklahoma. That kid stands six foot four, if he's an inch. He weighs two hundred and forty pounds and can run and root like a razorback hog. He's the prettiest sight you ever did see, Jack. I'd love to see him against those pretty boys down at Norman."

"I went to Stillwater for a game while I was in

Oklahoma. That little town comes alive when the college plays the university."

"It shore does," Clyde agreed. "Not even a good rodeo can stir the people up like that game."

"Do you think we could pull in an Oklahoma station if we put up a pretty good sized antenna? I doubt any of the games will be broadcast over the Anchorage station."

"I don't know, Jack. They've a powerful station in Tulsa. It'd be worth a try."

"We'll have to see what we can do about it, Clyde. And thanks for bringing down our dinner. Tell Bonnie thanks, too."

"Hey, now. That's okay, Jack. Glad to do it. It'll be great having another man around. Mike gets calls and is away a lot. I know ya'all ain't wantin' this old cowboy a hanging around so I'll just vamoose. Night, Jack. Thanks for the drink. Night, Kelly."

Kelly, who had kept herself busy at the stove so she wouldn't have to look at him, called out, "Night, Clyde." She didn't speak again until she heard the car door slam and the motor start. Finally, she turned to see Jonathan looking at her.

"I suppose you're pretty pleased with yourself," she sneered. "Clyde wasn't any challenge, at all. You charm men like him every day back in Boston!"

"Don't be nasty, Kelly."

"Poor Clyde was just an obstacle to overcome in

your own cold-blooded, calculated way." She laughed sardonically.

A faint red stain ran along his hard cheekbones. "Think what you like," he said, and poured himself a drink from the bottle of Scotch.

CHAPTER FIVE

THE MEAL TASTED like ashes in Kelly's mouth. She sat across the table from Jonathan and never once let her gaze rest on his face. Her depression deepened.

"You look worn out. You've been working too hard."

Kelly flushed and ignored him.

"You've lost weight."

"Well, what did you expect? I'm hardly the Boston debutante," she snapped.

She could feel his eyes on her. "Thank God, you're not. But you could try to be cordial, at least. You look as if you expect to be executed," he said through his teeth.

She gave him a false, over-bright smile. "You want me to look like this? I'll smile like a lighthouse, if that's what you want. You're the man in charge. You command, I obey."

His eyes flashed angrily. "One of these days you're going to push me too far."

"And you'll get nasty? You mean nastier than usual?"

Jonathan laid down his fork very carefully and the anger in his eyes intensified. "Stop the sarcasm, Kelly. You and I will be living here together and I've no intention of spending the winter sparring with you."

"You know the alternative."

Without answering, he began eating again—several helpings of the casserole and a large piece of pie. Kelly pushed her food around on her plate, knowing she should eat but not liking the feel of the food in her mouth. Instead, she drank several cups of coffee and rested her elbows on the table.

When Jonathan finished, he took his plate to the sink. Kelly scraped hers into a pan for Charlie, added the leftover casserole to it, and went to the door. Charlie bounded in the moment she opened it. He stood looking at Jonathan, then finally dropped the battered frisbee and, with a wag of his tail, began to gulp down the food. As he licked the pan clean, he moved it farther and farther into the room until it came up against Jonathan's foot. Charlie looked up at him and gave a low growl. Surprised, Kelly burst into peals of laughter.

"Charlie! You uncouth dog! You're not supposed to growl at Jonathan Winslow Templeton the Third. You're supposed to grovel at his feet." Kelly knew it was the Scotch talking, but she didn't care. "Be nice to him, Charlie, and he'll have a nice, big bone flown in from Boston." She poured another drink.

While she was washing the dishes, she had two more drinks and only vaguely heard Jonathan talking to Charlie and shutting the door after letting him out. She saw the hand reach out and take the bottle of Scotch and set it on the top shelf in the cabinet. She wanted to giggle. Did he think she wouldn't reach up and get it if she wanted more? She left the dishes on the drainboard and walked on unsteady legs to the door of her bedroom. With one hand on the doorframe to steady herself, she turned and tried to focus her eyes on Jonathan's face.

"I'm going to bed," she enunciated very clearly. "You can do as you please. Sleep on the couch or in my father's bed, if you can find blankets." She giggled and put her hand to her mouth. "Or sleep out in the snow with Charlie." Waving her hand carelessly, she swayed, then turned to go, but her feet wouldn't move. Jonathan caught her as she fell forward, his hands under her armpits. "I'm not sleeping with you. Do you hear? I hate the sight of you. Stay, if you've no more pride than to stay where you're not wanted, but you'll not get any pleasure out of my company!" The words had been burning in her head all evening and now they shot out at a frantic rate, clear and unwavering. She tried to stand up straight and push his hands away from her.

"You've had too much to drink," he said, apparently amused.

"Which is no business of yours." Her head was whirling and she found herself leaning against him for support. She closed her eyes. "Oh, my head!" she groaned.

He lifted her as if she weighed no more than a feather. Her head was swimming dizzily and she couldn't focus her eyes. She was only half aware that he was carrying her, then he lowered her to something soft and comfortable. She wanted to sleep, but his movements irritated her. Dimly she felt her shoes being removed and then her jeans. She tried to push him away when he lifted her to slip the shirt off her back. At last she was allowed to lay back and he covered her with something soft and warm. Almost instantly she was asleep.

During the night she began to dream lovely, wonderful, intensely exciting dreams. She was back with Jack in the king-sized bed at Captain Cook's Hotel in Anchorage, where they had spent the first two days after their marriage. She was submitting to his lovemaking, burning pleasurably under the smooth caress of his hands. The warmth of his body seemed to melt hers so that it molded to his shape. The dream was so deeply real she could feel his fingers on her bare skin searching for all the sensitive places and finding them.

She moaned aloud as his lips explored the warm curve of her throat and descended to the rounded flesh of her breast, fondling the stiff peaks until she turned her face into his neck and kissed his damp skin.

"Kiss me, darling," he breathed in her ear. "Kiss me and love me."

"Yes! Oh, yes!" Her lips, warm and eager, sought his that were firm, yet gentle, hardening with passion only at her insistence. Her hand stroked his wide chest, dark with rough hairs, and moved down to the flat, smooth-skinned stomach. Sensuous, languid, she took her time and explored his body boldly, giving herself up to this wonderful dream. "Jack . . . Jack . . ."

His mouth silenced hers and his palms moved down over her body and curved against her hips. He whispered love words in her ear and she felt his cheek against her breast. And then his mouth slid gently over the white skin until it enclosed her nipple. He repeated the caress, his mouth seductive, lazy, setting her ablaze with hunger. He was invading every inch of her now, exploring her body boldly, making her give herself up to him. He began to kiss her mouth deeply and Kelly slid her arms around his neck and pulled on the hair on the back of his head. His breath came fast and thick, hers light and gasping.

"Say you love me." The husky whisper in her ear was insistent. "Say it, darling."

"I love you, Jack. Jack, love me. Love me."

The laugh was low and tender as he covered her

face with feverish kisses. "Oh, Kelly," he said thickly. "You've been under my skin for so long, tormenting me, driving me crazy. I've missed you so and I've wanted to make love to you for so long . . ." He pulled her head back and their mouths clung. He held her body between his roving hands and she made no effort to stop him. The pleasure rose to intolerable heights and she lost consciousness of everything but the powerful body that was driving her toward weightlessness. Now she was floating down from a great height and her stomach clenched in fierce panic. She dropped sharply, and cried out wildly, her hands clinging frantically to the only solid thing in her tilting world.

Soothing words calmed and reassured her. Hands gently stroked her taut body. Her heart settled in to a quieter pace as the tension and panic left her. Did he know he had taken her heart? She began to cry. Jack had taken her heart, but Jonathan had taken and crushed her bubbly spirit, her romantic illusions. She had fought to hold Jack, but in the end he had flown from her grasp. Now, like the princess in the fairy tale, she was under the spell of the wicked prince, Jonathan, who would destroy her. Finally her sleep deepened and the nightmare left her.

The sensation of something against her mouth woke her abruptly. Her eyes flew open and stared into amused brown eyes. She was lying naked in

Jonathan's arms, her legs imprisoned between his. He had been kissing her. He laughed at the expression on her face. There was a relaxed charm about him that maddened her. His hand was on her breast, fingering her nipple!

Her face burned scarlet. She hadn't been dreaming! She had made love with him! "Oh! You're even lower than I thought!" She tried to push him away, but her strength was as nothing against his. "You . . . you took my clothes off!"

"You didn't object at the time," he pointed out with a grin that further infuriated her.

"I didn't know . . . You took advantage . . ."

"You were plastered," he interrupted, grinning.

"You had no right. You knew I didn't want you," she snapped.

"I had every right . . . and you did want me."

She shook her head like an enraged child, her face livid. "I did not want you, Jonathan!" She began to struggle.

He clamped his arms and legs around her and lowered his lips to her cheek. "You wanted Jack. It was just like those two days we spent in bed after we got married . . . only better."

Her eyes burned up at him resentfully. "Enjoy your little triumph. It won't happen again."

"Be honest. Your appetite for me is as great as mine is for you." His hands moved possessively over her, his fingers trembling. "You can feel how I want you. Admit you want me, too."

"I admit I enjoy being with a man. Any man," she taunted.

His hand moved to her hair and jerked her head around to face him. "That's a lie!" he said harshly. He looked at her mouth, that trembling mouth that had always fascinated him. "Your mouth is too beautiful to spit such lies." He kissed it gently before his lips hovered over hers so that his tongue could trace its way into the corners. "You're a lovely liar," he said, his eyes soft, his hands gentle in her hair. "Don't be embarrassed for wanting me, darling."

She felt as though he had penetrated her subconscious and raped her mind as well as her body. She must have been conscious at some level to remember what he had done to her and how his stroking hands had fired her desire for him. But she feared her blind, desperate need for love. It was too dangerous to care for anyone.

"Sex!" The word exploded from her and her eyes filled with tears. "That's all it is, Jonathan. Let me go, please. I want to get up," she said tiredly.

"Maybe it is just sex, but it's a start," he said patiently and moved away from her.

Kelly threw back the covers and walked naked into the bathroom. She could feel his eyes on her, but didn't care. She remembered the long nights during the first weeks of their marriage when Jack's passion, the force of which carried her over the first few times when she bared her body to him, made her feel as if it was natural and beautiful for him to view her from every angle.

She took her robe from the hook behind the door, slipped her feet into warm scuffs, and passed through her father's room to come out into the living area. It was warm. A big log blazed in the fireplace and the cookstove was roaring pleasantly. She glanced toward the door. The floor and doormat were dry. Since no one had come in from outside, Jonathan must have built up the fire. She was surprised he knew how. She filled the coffee pot and set it on the stove. During the few short weeks she had been home, she had fallen into a routine: get up, stoke up the fires, put on the coffee pot, wind the clock, turn on the electric hot water tank. She did these things, now, automatically, and went to stand beside the window.

It was going to be a clear day with a blue sky. Soon the sun would be up, its low rays bathing the landscape in a warm, winter-rose color.

She loved this land of the very old and the very new. Ancient Eskimo and Indian cultures lived side by side with modern pulp mills, fisheries, and giant oil companies. Where else in the world were there glaciers and strawberries, dog teams and airplanes, skin boats (the design of which had not changed for a thousand years) and late model outboard motors? It seemed ironic that she and Jonathan should come together in this land of extremes.

The day promised to be clear enough to allow the first guests to view Mount McKinley from the lodge windows. Kelly thought of the poster she had painstakingly printed and framed to hang beside the window. "Mount McKinley, called *Denali*, meaning 'home of the sun,' by the Indians, is one of the most dramatic sights in Alaska. The light tan granite mass, crown of the Alaska Range, climbs upward to a height of almost four miles. No other mountain rises so far above its own base. The upper two-thirds of the peak is permanently snow-covered, and often takes on a pinkish glow at sunrise and sunset."

Thinking about the mighty mountain, this place her father had built, this home she loved, stiffened her resolve to stay here. She would not let Jonathan evict her and Mike and Marty from their home! They belonged here, he didn't.

Kelly turned from the window to see him taking coffee cups from the drain-basket beside the sink. She looked at him with new eyes. He wore a flannel shirt, obviously new, jeans, and wool socks on his feet. Dressed like this, he seemed more Jack than Jonathan, but he *was* Jonathan, and he could take all this away from her. She picked up her purse from the couch and took out her cigarettes and lighter.

"When did you start smoking?" He had poured two cups of coffee and set them on the table.

"I don't smoke much. Only when I'm nervous," she retorted.

"You're nervous now?"

"Wouldn't you be if everything you loved could be taken from you on a whim?"

He stood looking at her. He seemed taller in the jeans, tall and tough, a bargaining Bostonian with an eye to the main chance, even willing to dress the part in order to fit into the scheme of things.

His dark eyes flickered with annoyance, but he spoke calmly. "I haven't threatened to take your home away from you."

She shrugged. "Same thing. I either suffer your presence or Marty and Mike and I get out."

"I doubt if you suffer, Kelly," he said drily. "Come drink your coffee."

"Thank you, no. I'll take my bath now. I only run the electric heater long enough to get water for a bath. Electricity is expensive here. Of course, you'd know nothing about that." She flicked the end of her cigarette into the fireplace and glanced at him. He sat at the table, stirring his coffee.

The C.B. radio came on with an emergency call for Mike. Kelly waited until she heard Mike answer, then went into the bathroom and filled the small tub with warm water.

When she came out of the warm, steamy bathroom, her bedroom seemed cold, but she shut the door connecting it to the kitchen and took out flannel-lined jeans and a shirt. Then she noticed her bed had been neatly made and the clothes she had worn the day before folded and laid out on the end. She dressed, ran a comb through her hair, and went in her stocking feet to the kitchen. She was pouring coffee when Jonathan came to the door of her father's room.

"Are you feeling better . . . besides being nervous?" he asked drily.

"Much better." There was almost a pleasant tone to her voice. "You'll find sheets and blankets in the chest at the end of the bed."

"I saw them there," he said, and turned back into the room.

Kelly carried her coffee to the kitchen window and looked out at the large temperature gage attached to a post just outside the window. It was eighteen degrees, about average for this time of year. There was no wind and the snow was fresh and beautiful. It was a perfect day for their guests to arrive. She hurriedly finished her coffee and put on her boots, coat, and yellow cap.

Charlie greeted her the moment she stepped outside. He had made crazy patterns in the snow and now leaped joyously. Kelly took the frisbee from him and sailed it into the air. The soft snow floated around him like a cloud as he dashed and leaped to catch it. She couldn't hold back her laughter.

"Charlie, you crazy dog! Come on, bring it here."

Shaking his head, as if the frisbee in his mouth was a live thing, he trotted back to Kelly. She knelt in the snow and put her arms about his neck, then took the frisbee from him and ran. Charlie was surprised at first then leaped after her, jumping high in the air when she held his toy over her head.

"No, you don't!" Kelly laughed, and tried to hit him on the nose. Charlie snapped at the battered plastic, braced his legs and pulled. Kelly went tumbling down into the snow, where she lay laughing, holding onto the frisbee with both hands. Charlie pulled and shook his head, deep growls coming from his powerful throat.

"Looks like a standoff to me."

Kelly looked up to see Jonathan standing over her, his hands deep in the pockets of his jacket. His gaze was so quiet and so penetrating that it seemed to reach down inside her. She felt something twist in her body and bit down on her lower lip. She let go of the frisbee and a surprised Charlie sat down in the snow.

Kelly got to her feet and brushed the snow from her jacket and jeans.

"I didn't mean to spoil your fun," Jonathan said from behind her.

"You didn't." The lie came easily to her lips. She headed toward the lodge. The light snow made walking easy, now; later it would be hard and crusty, then solid enough to walk on.

Jonathan followed beside her. As they neared the lodge, he took hold of her arm and held tightly when she tried to shrug it off.

"Let go of my arm," she said tensely, glancing up at him.

"No." He held her gaze as firmly as her arm. "Behave yourself, Kelly. I won't be snubbed by my wife in front of anyone. Do you understand?" He took a deep breath, his nostrils flaring. "What we say and do is one thing in private and another in public."

Tormented, she tried without success to break free of his hold. "I have my pride, too," she retorted. "I won't play the loving wife!"

"If you don't, you'll only make matters worse for yourself."

"Worse! How can matters be worse than they are?" she hissed.

"Believe me, they could be much worse."

They had reached the door and Jonathan held it open for her. Needing a chance to pull herself back together after their verbal combat, she took an unusually long time pulling off her boots and leaving them on the mat. She allowed him to help her with her jacket, then went toward the swinging doors leading to the kitchen. Half of her wanted to watch his reaction to the lodge; the other half wanted him to think she didn't care a fig.

"There you are! I swear to goodness, I told

Clyde we just might not see you all day. I know how it was when me and Clyde got together after we was apart." Bonnie wiped her hands on her apron and held one of them out to Jonathan. "Now ain't you a handsome feller? You rascal," she said to Kelly. "You never told me nothin' about a husband. If mine was as handsome as yours, I'd a been braggin' all over the place."

Jonathan laughed. "Kelly didn't think I'd be able to get away so soon, Bonnie. That's why she didn't tell you about me."

"I know she's tickled you're here now. Married folks was meant to be together. I ain't for this woman libbers stuff. I want my man to lean on. Ain't that right, Kelly?"

Kelly found her voice. "Oh, yes. Jonathan's a pillar of strength."

"Jonathan? Clyde said your name was Jack." Bonnie looked up from her scant five feet to the man towering over her.

"That's right. My name's Jack. Only Kelly calls me Jonathan and that's only part of the time." His brown eyes glinted into her stormy blue ones. The look passed over Bonnie, who was waddling back to the stove in her fur-lined moccasins.

"I just fed Mike and sent him on his way." Bonnie moved the big iron skillet onto the hot part of the range. "I swear if that kid's legs ain't holler. Ain't one blessed thing wrong with his appetite. He ate three eggs, sausage, and hash browns, then topped it off with the last of the pie. What you gonna have, Jack?"

"I'll take the same, Bonnie, but make it two eggs."

"Over easy or wide awake?"

"If wide awake means sunny side up, that's how I'll take them."

"Well, get on over here and get you some coffee. Get some for Kelly, too. She looks all tuckered out. Skinny as a rail, that girl. Now that you're here, Jack, maybe we can fatten her up a little." Bonnie dropped big pats of sausage into the hot skillet. "She's worn herself out working around here. My land, you should've seen the mess this place was in. There wasn't anything too heavy for her to lift, and nothing too hard for her to do. She just flew right in there and did it and wouldn't wait one minute for the men. Mike takes things slow an' easy. That boy don't get in no hurry. He . . . Put the bread in the toaster, Jack."

Kelly closed her eyes in frustration. "Mike works hard," she said.

"I didn't say he didn't work, Kelly. I just said he was slow. Swear, if you ain't somethin' when it comes to stickin' up for that boy!"

"I'd hardly call him a boy, Bonnie," Kelly said drily and raised her eyes to see Jonathan watching her, the smile he had worn for Bonnie's benefit gone. "Mike has done a lot of work around here," she said, holding Jonathan's eyes. "He's never had anything

84

given to him. He earned his share of this place."

"I'm sure he did. Now that I'm here, I can take some of the work load off his shoulders." Jonathan's voice was kind, but his face was not. Kelly knew he was furious and was glad.

The plate of food Bonnie set in front of her caused Kelly's stomach to lurch with hunger. She glanced up to see Jonathan's brows rise questioningly. She could tell he was enjoying her discomfort.

"Not hungry this morning, darling?" he asked silkily.

Her eyes, filled with rage, flashed to his face. He returned the look with taunting amusement. The battle lines were drawn, she thought bitterly. She was bound to lose some of the encounters, but she was determined to win the war.

CHAPTER SIX

I am the captain of my fate. The thought pounded in Kelly's head while she went through the motions of checking the guest rooms to make sure everything was ready. In the middle of counting the number of extra blankets neatly stacked on a closet shelf, she stopped, put her clenched fists to her temples, and closed her eyes.

It was ridiculous to think she was captain of anything, least of all her own fate! She was being swept along on the tide of Jonathan's overpowering personality. Already Bonnie and Clyde thought he was the greatest thing since fire. He was out there now, on one end of the big, two-man crosscut saw, helping Clyde cut the big logs into lengths to be further chopped into firewood. Kelly hoped Clyde worked him to death. She knew Jonathan would be too proud to stop even if he was about to drop in his tracks.

Kelly stayed at the lodge until the guests arrived, leaving only long enough to go to her own house and change into azure blue cord slacks and a matching turtleneck sweater that hid some of the gauntness of her slim hips. Clyde left in plenty of time to meet the train and Jonathan, taking his cue from Kelly, came up to the lodge after changing out of the sawdust-covered jeans and sweaty flannel shirt. He had bathed, and Kelly wondered if he had used cold water, or if he had carried it from the reservoir beside the cookstove. He had put on tan trousers and a brown loose-knit shirt with cream ribbing at the neck and cuffs.

He came to where Kelly was standing beside the window looking out toward the faint peak of Mount McKinley. She could smell the familiar aroma of his aftershave lotion. He didn't speak and she moved away to turn on the lamps. It was three o'clock in the afternoon and already begin-ning to get dark. Soon they would be using elec-tricity all day and the bills would pile up.

The guests were young, rowdy, and there were

five of them instead of four. The girls had frizzed hair, thinly plucked eyebrows, and willowy figures once they removed their bulky snowmobile wear. The men had fashionably styled haircuts and expensive Nordic ski sweaters. Clyde set their suitcases inside the door, but when he started to remove his boots to carry the luggage to the rooms, Jonathan stopped him.

"I'll take care of that, Clyde, if you want to put the car away."

It was easy to tell what girl went with what man. One of the couples was rather short, the other of medium height. The odd man was taller and older than the others. He leaned on the small bar that served as a counter and eyed Kelly.

"Hello, snow-nymph. I don't have a reservation. Are you going to throw me out?" His eyes ran over her like summer rain.

"That depends." Kelly saw Jonathan edge closer to the desk.

"Yeah? On what?" He looked intrigued.

"On whether or not you behave youself." Her eyes glinted mischievously. He wasn't the enemy, just a harmless man who liked to flirt. He looked like a nice guy.

"May I ask you a crazy question?" He grinned broadly.

"Sure. What's the crazy question?"

"What's a classy looking dame like you doing out here in the boonies?"

Kelly laughed. "That line went out with hula-hoops and mini-skirts." She pushed the register toward him. "Sign your name and next of kin in case I decide to feed you to the bears."

Doctor Andrew T. Mullins, Seattle, Washington. Without allowing a flicker of surprise to show on her face, she moved the book toward the other guests.

"We have three private rooms and a dormitory," Kelly explained, looking at the tall doctor.

"We'll take the three privates," he said and threw a credit card down on the counter.

"You don't need to pay now." Kelly handed the card back to him and he squeezed her fingers.

"Going to run up the bill on me?" he teased.

"Hope so," she retorted, and glanced at Jonathan.

He stood behind the other couples, his eyes riveted to her, his face a frowning mask. There was no doubt he was angry. He watched her with barely controlled impatience, his body shifting restlessly.

"Dinner's at seven, but the coffee pot is always on. The swinging doors lead to the dining area, which is also the kitchen. This is a very informal lodge so make yourselves at home."

Kelly almost broke into a grin when she saw Jonathan carrying the luggage down the hall. If only Katherine were here to see it! As the tall doctor turned to go, he winked at her and, feeling Jonathan's eyes on her, she winked back.

In moments Jonathan returned from the bedrooms. "Pull another stunt like that," he warned her, "and I'll break your neck!"

"What are you talking about?" Kelly demanded, goading him.

He slammed his hand down on the desk. "You know very well what I'm talking about. That was a come-on if I ever saw one." His hand snaked out and grabbed her wrist.

Her face turned pale and their eyes locked in silent battle. Damn him! He was going to push, push, push, until he drove her out of her mind!

"Give up, Jonathan. Go back to your tinfoil world, your elegant papier-mâché friends and their lifeless parties, where they cut each other's throats so politely. I don't need you here." She was surprised she could speak so calmly. Suddenly pale and haggard, he stared back as if he wasn't seeing her at all. She jerked her hand free and headed for the kitchen.

"We have an extra guest, Bonnie," she announced, taking a mug from the rack and pouring coffee as Jonathan followed through the swinging doors.

"Ain't that great? I peeked when I heard 'em come in. Tonight we're goin' to have chicken fricassee and dumplins. Don't that sound fancy? Kelly, get Jack a cup of coffee. That boy worked like a mule this mornin'."

"Keep your seat, I'll get it." He laid his hand on

her shoulder as he passed and Kelly steeled herself to keep from flinching.

"If you're hungry, Jack, get yourself a piece of that carrot cake," Bonnie ordered. "We're goin' to have baked custard tonight along with the French rolls, peas and onions in cream, and tossed salad."

"Sounds good, Bonnie. Do you ever make Boston baked beans?" Jack glanced at Kelly and grinned. "My wife never learned to like them."

"I make Oklahoma beans and they'd put them Boston beans to shame, Jack. I don't blame Kelly none for not likin' 'em." Bonnie waddled between the stove and the counter, never glancing at the two seated at the trestle table. "One of these days I'll cook up a batch of pinto beans, tomatoes, and *jalapeño* peppers. Top that off with a pan of good, old yellow cornbread and you never had anything so good in all your life." Bonnie went into the pantry.

"We know what's on the menu. What's on the program for tonight?" Jonathan asked.

Kelly let out a deep sigh. It was so exhausting to be always sparring with him. As he turned to see if Bonnie was coming back into the room, she regarded him openly. His sharply etched profile seemed to be carved from granite. He was handsome, strong and ruthless. Here, in the Alaskan wilderness, he seemed to take on a ruggedly masculine appearance totally different from the suave, socially prominent man of Boston. There was no doubt he stirred her physically. But did she feel love or hate?

His brown eyes held a question when he swung around to her, and she gave an involuntary shiver. What did he want from her? He had no need for a woman's enduring love. With that arrogant face, imperious head, and cultured background, he could get any woman he wanted. She put her hand to her breast as if to press her heart into obedience. She didn't want to love him. She wanted to be her own woman, not chained to him by the strength of her feelings.

Now his fingers locked about her wrist, making a double shackle. "Kelly, what's wrong?"

She flinched as if his words were razor sharp. "What could possibly be wrong?" she asked flippantly. "I've got the world by the tail going downhill backwards!" She felt as brittle as breaking glass. She wanted to cry for all those lovely nights so long ago when she'd been young and in love.

"Break . . . break. . . . Mobile one calling Mountain View base station." Mike's voice came in on the radio and Jonathan gave a muffled curse.

Kelly pressed the button on the microphone. "Mountain View, go ahead."

"Is that you, Ramblin' Rose?"

"Ten-four. You got the Ramblin' Rose."

"You got the Barefoot Renegade on this end."

"No kidding! I thought I had the president of Mobile Oil. What's your ten-twenty, Barefoot?"

91

"I'm out here on this ice-covered drag-strip heading for Hurricane. I've got a call to make there and may not make it back to the lodge tonight. I didn't want you to worry about me."

Kelly darted a glance at Jonathan, whose sharp eyes watched every move she made. She knew Mike wanted to spite Jonathan. She felt like a bone between two dogs.

"Ten-four, good buddy. Keep the rubber side down and I'll catch you on the flip-flop. This Ramblin' Rose will be clear."

"Bye, Rose. This Barefoot Renegade is . . . ga— on!"

Kelly looked up to see Jonathan raise his eyes to the ceiling in disgust. Her own eyes lit up and a giggle escaped her lips.

"What's the matter, Jonathan? Too much corn? We'll have to find a C.B. handle for you. Let's see, you could be the Boston Bean!" She felt deliciously wicked. Her blue eyes danced and her delicate mouth smiled mischievously. "Break . . . break for the Boston Bean. Are you on the channel, Bean?"

She didn't know what to expect from her teasing but didn't care. Under her gaze his hard features softened and his lips turned up. Finally he broke into a wide grin. They sat looking into each other's eyes and Kelly's thoughts were blown from her like leaves before a wind.

"Ten-four, Ramblin' Rose, you got the Bean." Had he really said that?

Kelly burst out laughing. Jack watched her in silence, a gentle smile flitting across his lips.

"Can you imagine Katherine's reaction to that?" She leaned forward, her eyes glinting between dark lashes. "She'd insist on Boston Bean, Esquire!" She propped her elbow on the table and cupped her chin in her hand, trying to surpress her giggles.

"Jack!" Bonnie's voice came from deep within the pantry. "Would ya help me get this box off the shelf? When God passed out arms, he gave me the leftovers!"

Reluctantly, Jonathan got to his feet, his eyes still on Kelly. There was nothing arrogant or frightening about him now.

"Jack!"

Jonathan muttered an oath. Then, "Kelly?"

"What do you want?"

He leaned over and kissed her on the cheek. "Thank you."

"What for?"

"For letting me have a glimpse of the Kelly I fell in love with two years ago."

Her face paled. Fear closed like a cold hand around her heart. She was furious with herself for letting down the barrier. All he needed was one little crack in the armor she had built around herself and he would work his way into her heart again.

"No! That Kelly is dead. I'm no longer the stupid, naive person you met in Anchorage."

"Jack!"

"Damn!" he muttered and turned toward the pantry.

"Watch it . . . Jack." Her taunting words dripped with sarcasm. "Your image is slipping."

His face was unreadable, and she wondered if her jeeringly spoken words had upset him. She felt uneasy beneath his stare and hurriedly looked away when she saw his face harden and a muscle jerk beside his mouth.

Dinner that evening was lively and amusing. Bonnie had covered the long trestle table with a blue denim cloth and served the food on heavy, white plates. An oil lamp, its glass chimney sparkling, stood in the middle of the table surrounded by bowls of deliciously cooked food. The guests, enjoying the homey atmosphere, kept up a lively conversation while Bonnie, dressed all in red with her bleached hair piled haphazardly on top of her head, kept the table supplied with hot rolls straight from the oven.

Kelly noted that the silence between her and Jonathan seemed to pass more or less unnoticed. She watched the pretty blonde with large breasts flirt openly with him, her heavily coated lashes brushing against her cheeks. The girl was blatantly eager but her companion merely transferred his attention to the other woman of the party. The two remaining males concentrated on Kelly, giving her little time to analyze her feelings when the blonde looped her arm through Jonathan's. They all passed through the swinging doors into the main room, where Clyde had built up a cheerful fire and Lawrence Welk music was coming from the stereo.

"My favorite music!" The tall doctor slipped his arm around Kelly and began to dance.

"Liar. You don't look like the Lawrence Welk type to me." Kelly followed his lead around the room, her hand on his broad shoulder.

"No? What type am I? Willie Nelson?" He held her away and smiled.

"I'd say you're more the Beach Boys type."

"How did you know?" He began to sing and whirled her around the room.

She laughed. "Stop it, you're making me dizzy!" Out of the corner of her eye she noticed two other couples dancing. Jonathan was standing with his back to the fireplace watching them.

"Your husband is watching us. Do you mind?"

"How did you know he's my husband?"

"He told me when he brought in the luggage." He held her away again to look down into her face. "Something tells me your marriage is on the rocks."

She looked up at him in surprise, then stiffened. "Something tells me it's none of your business!" Pain made her voice harsh.

"Oops! I put my foot in, didn't I? You're not

quite over him, yet. Breaking up is hard to do, but you'll survive. Take it from me. It'll be easier if you send him packing, or else split from this place."

"I don't recall asking your advice," Kelly said coolly. "Now if you'll excuse me, I'll see about setting up a game table for my other guests."

"Games? Great idea. How about spin the bottle, or button, button who's got the button, or . . . strip poker?" He grinned and she had to laugh. It was impossible to be angry at him for long.

"Come help me set up the table. Do you play Scrabble?"

"If you let me use dirty words."

"Are you ever serious? What kind of a doctor are you?"

"I specialize in female sexual problems."

"Are you kidding?"

"Yes. I'm a foot doctor."

Later, Kelly learned Andy was a general practitioner and had given up a lucrative practice in Seattle to become resident doctor on an Indian reservation in Washington. This was his first vacation in two years, and he had come to Anchorage to attend a seminar and to visit his sister.

As the evening wore on, Kelly found herself becoming tense at the realization that she would have to go back to the cabin with Jonathan. Even as she was trying to think of a reason not to leave, Jonathan was explaining that Bonnie and Clyde were in the room off the kitchen. If they wanted anything, they need only ring the bell on the desk.

"Breakfast will be served anytime before noon," he concluded, holding Kelly's jacket for her to slip into. "We'll see you in the morning." He ushered her out the door before she could say goodnight.

The night seemed bitterly cold after the warmth of the lodge. Kelly eased down the icy steps, shrugging off the hand Jonathan offered. She refused to admire the beauty of the moonlight on the fresh snow or the dark, drooping evergreens that stood like proud sentinels around the resort buildings. She walked ahead of him toward her home, lost in disturbing thoughts. They reached the cabin and Jonathan opened the door and switched on the light before moving aside for Kelly to enter.

"I won't be so optimistic as to expect a few quiet moments with my wife before our own hearth." He helped her with her coat and removed his own.

She prickled with annoyance at his tone. "I'm having a cup of hot chocolate."

"Sounds good. I haven't had a cup of chocolate in years."

"Why not? Too busy drinking tea?" Even as she said it, she wanted to take it back. She glanced at him. He had settled down on the couch and extended his stocking feet toward the blaze.

"The boarding school where I lived didn't offer chocolate, so I never acquired a taste for it."

"How long did you live at the boarding school?" Kelly asked, pouring milk into a pan on the stove.

"Until I went to college."

Kelly was about to ask, what college, but she knew it would be Harvard, Princeton, or Yale, so she didn't bother. She lapsed into silence, thinking how little she knew about this man she had married. She stirred cocoa and sugar into the hot milk and poured the steaming liquid into mugs, then carried one to Jonathan and seated herself in the rocker, nursing her own mug in both hands.

"Isn't it time we started to get to know each other? It seems absurd that we've been married for two years without knowing the first thing about what makes each other tick," he said softly. "Of course we've been together only a third of that time."

"I think you know everything there is to know about me." She wished he wouldn't keep looking at her.

"That's where you're wrong. I saw a completely different side of you today."

"So?" She shrugged and lapsed into silence.

"Talk to me, Kelly." The force of his voice betrayed his irritation.

"What about? You never told me much about yourself, either." She tried to make her voice casual, uncaring.

"It didn't seem relevant. I think you can sum up my life in two words . . . work and work. I've spent far too many hours working, or flying around the world working. When I wasn't working, I didn't know what to do with myself."

"Oh, I'm sure Katherine and Nancy could have thought of something."

He threw her a piercing look. "What do you mean by that?"

"Don't be stupid. I'm sure you know Nancy would have loved to help you relax." She got to her feet.

"A remark like that almost makes me think you're jealous."

She stared in blank bewilderment, then jerked the empty mug from his hand. "Fun—ny!" She set the mugs on the table and opened the glass door of the mantel clock and began to wind the spring.

"Getting late, is it?" Jonathan asked in a sardonic tone.

"Yes, and I want to get to bed," she snapped.

"So do I," he said softly, and her face burned.

To cover her confusion, she tried to lift a large chunk of wood and put it on the fireplace grate. It slipped in her hands, the rough wood tearing at her palms and ripping a fingernail. She could have bitten her tongue for allowing the small cry to escape her lips. Jonathan was by her side instantly, taking the heavy log from her hands. He threw it on the grate and shoved it in place with the fire-tongs. By the time he turned, Kelly was halfway to the bedroom door.

"Kelly, wait. Let me see your hand."

"It's only a scratch," she said over her shoulder.

"I want to see for myself. I think it's more than a mere scratch."

She turned on him like a spitting cat. "Bug off, Jonathan. I've about had all of you I can take. Leave me alone!" In her anguish she felt herself losing control.

He searched her features intently. "All right, Kelly. I won't bother you if you'd rather be alone. I was concerned for you and wanted to help if I could."

Tears filled Kelly's eyes. She'd been prepared for bitterness but not kindness. She fled to her room before the tears could fall.

CHAPTER SEVEN

KELLY COULDN'T HELP SHIVERING. The look in Jonathan's eyes as she turned away from him made her afraid—not of him, but of herself. She hated him, hated her own weakness for him. Her head started whirling dizzily. Her breathing quickened and a longing almost like a pain washed over her—a longing for that time long ago when she and Mike and Marty had been young and silly. When the only problems they'd had were getting the latest Beatles record or enough gas in the truck to go to Talkeetna.

She walked slowly into the bathroom, catching a glimpse of herself in the mirror. She paused. It was like seeing someone else. Her body looked the same, but her face was empty. She felt as if she didn't belong to herself. She wanted to laugh, she wanted to cry. Tears won.

"You're dumb, Kelly!" she muttered. "You're dumb and stupid. You've not only screwed up your own life, you've ruined things for Mike and Marty as well."

The palm of her hand began to sting and she went to the bathroom in search of medication. She felt so lonely, so lost, so frantic.

She heard Jonathan moving about in the other bedroom and her heart gave a sudden sickening leap. She dabbed unnecessarily hard at the scratches on her palm where the red blood beaded. She knew and understood the bond that existed between her and Jonathan, just as she knew that the almost unbearable longing that swept her at times was more than a mere physical longing, but a yearning to belong, to have someone of her very own. She shook her head, trying to force herself to remember her true motive for leaving him, to steel herself against the dangerous knowledge that he was scarcely twenty feet away and his lips, his arms, his masculinity could engulf her and carry her away to forgetfulness. To give way to the treachery of such thoughts could only lead to more heartbreak. A shudder ran through her. With trembling fingers she replaced the bottle in the medicine cabinet. Jonathan was a taker. He would take all she had to give and her own need, her pride, would be wiped away like so many snowflakes on a hot stove.

She cleaned her face, brushed her teeth, and glanced about to make sure the bathroom was tidy before she left it. In her bedroom she put on her warm flannel nightgown and put away her slacks and sweater. After turning down her bed, she switched off the lamp and went to open the door leading into the living room.

She wasn't ready to confront him again so soon, but there he was, framed in the doorway. The light was behind him and she couldn't see the expression on his face. But she could feel his eyes, so disturbingly intent, on her.

"It isn't going to work, you know!" she flung at him belligerently.

"Is your hand all right?"

"Yes!" Kelly was irritated that he could stand there so calmly while she felt as if she would fly into a million pieces.

"Get into bed and I'll bring you a hot drink." He spoke as if to a rebellious child.

"I don't believe you! You can't be real!" she wailed. "Can't you see I don't want you here? You have absolutely no right to interfere in my life.

You really are something else, Jonathan. I can't find a word to describe you . . ." She was ashamed of the silly, childish words that tumbled from her mouth.

She began to shake uncontrollably and wasn't sure if it was from the cold or because her nerves were so strung out. She flung herself back into the darkened room with head bowed, slid into bed, and tried to tuck her cold feet up into the warm folds of her nightgown. She was paying the price for those few blissful weeks when her love for him had consumed her and she had allowed him to take over her life.

Jonathan came to stand beside the bed but she ignored him.

"Turn over, Kelly. I've brought you a hot drink." When she refused to move, he placed his hand on her shoulder. "You're shaking like a leaf. Turn over and drink this. It's only whiskey and a little sugar and hot water. It'll warm you up."

Kelly turned over, sat up, and almost snatched the mug from his hand. Anything to get rid of him, she told herself.

"Is there something that needs to be done aside from banking the fires?"

"No, but leave the doors open so the pipes don't freeze," she answered grudgingly.

"I'll take care of it." He took the empty cup from her hand, pushed her gently down into the bed and tucked the covers about her shoulders.

Her body was as taut as a bow-string and her limbs icy cold, but already warmth from the drink was beginning to penetrate her chilled body. She kept her eyes tightly closed, wishing desperately for sleep.

Cold air hit her in the back. The mattress sagged as Jonathan lowered his weight onto the bed. Her eyes flew open and she gave a high wail. Panic stricken, she flopped over to face him, then tried to back away.

"No! No, Jonathan. I won't sleep with you!" Her hands went to his chest to push him away from her. His skin was bare and warm and his masculine scent was so familiar! She smelled the mint of toothpaste on his breath when he leaned over her. Her heart beat with sheer horror. He was forging chains that were binding her to him. "Please! Please, don't." Her control broke and she begged pitilessly.

He ignored her pleas and pulled her to him, his muscled body free and unconfined. He searched and found her lips, opening them with the urgent pressure of his own. Her senses swam beneath his eager conquest. Pride forced her to continue to struggle in his arms and the gown worked up and over her thighs. Panic flared as he swung his bare leg over hers and held her softness pinned to the yielding mattress.

"You want me, darling!" he said slowly, his voice husky against her mouth. She tried to shake her head in silent denial, but he had locked it between his hands. "You want me as much as I want you." His tongue played with her lips.

"Wanting and loving are not the same," she gasped in a breathless whisper.

"Think of the wanting. The other can come later."

"No! I can't do it, Jonathan," she mumbled frantically.

"Jack. Think of me as the Jack you loved during those few wonderful weeks," he insisted.

"It makes no difference!"

"It does to me," he returned in that soft, seductive voice.

"No!" Even while she was protesting, her blood ran like liquid fire through her veins. His hand caressed her back, stroking away the flannel gown and running urgently over her smooth skin, caressing her into surrender. She tried to protest, "No . . ." but the word was muffled by the drugging seduction of his mouth against her own.

Again she tried to push him away, but he tilted her to him, making her helpless, while his lips deepened their kiss. Her hands moved to his smooth, thick hair and fondled his neck and the strong line of his shoulders and back, then came up to stroke his cheeks and caress his ears.

Jonathan let his mouth wander over her face. "Say it, Kelly. Say you want me, that you like the feel of my body against yours."

Refusing to answer, she struggled with the

weakness that swept over her. The sensual need she had been fighting was taking complete control of her. The power of the sexual drive she had suppressed and stifled for months swamped her, driving away all coherent thought except the one that told her she was doomed if she surrendered completely.

"Say it," he whispered in her ear.

"I can't! I can't!"

"Yes, you can. I'm not asking for your heart, but for the possession of your body. I won't force anything from you that you're not willing to give. I want to make love to you, and I know you want me too. There's no commitment, darling," he said in tense deliberation.

"No commitment? No! You want a woman and any woman will do! I won't be used!" She tried to scramble away from him.

"Darling," he groaned in protest, lifting his head and moving his body over hers to hold her, "that wasn't what I meant. You crazy girl . . . be still and let me love you."

Only later did Kelly pause to ask herself wildly what she was doing. She should be fighting him. Instead she wanted to feel his skin against hers. Obediently she raised her arms and allowed him to slip the nightgown over her head. Then she was in his embrace, his arms and legs locked around her and her breasts crushed against the fine cloud of hair on his chest.

"Sweetheart, you're so beautiful," he groaned in a husky voice. "Forget everything, but you and me and how I want to love you. You want me. . . . You do want me?" The muttered words were barely coherent, thickly groaned into her ear as he kissed the warm curve of her neck.

The deeply buried heat in her own body seemed to flare out of control, and she sought his mouth hungrily. Her hands moved to his back, digging into the smooth muscles. She felt the powerful tug of her own desire for him and admitted what her subconscious mind had known since the moment he came to the cabin. She wanted him.

He began to stroke her, whispering words, their meaning muffled for her as he kissed her soft, rounded breasts, nibbling with his teeth, nuzzling with his lips. He was totally absorbed in giving her pleasure and at the same time pleasing himself. She twisted and turned beneath him, bringing a groan of satisfaction to his lips. She was hungry for him, and returned his caresses with all the instinctive sexuality of her young body. Only Jack made love to her like this and he had been an expert teacher.

"Jack! Oh, Jack!" She arched her back, her senses surging to limitless peaks of pleasure. She was being carried on a tidal wave of desire.

"Darling, beautiful, Kelly," he breathed, his hands sliding down her spine to the provocative curve of her hips.

Their lovemaking was a devastating experience, and when it was over, he didn't move away from her. Instead, he cupped her face with his hands and sought her mouth with his.

"That was good, wasn't it?" he said huskily, running his mouth over her face. His lips paused to tease her lashes. "Kelly, Kelly. . . . How did I survive without you all those months? I love the feel of your breasts against me and the taste of your mouth. You're so soft, so feminine, so incredibly beautiful!"

Kelly lay tightly against his body, her head resting on his chest. She couldn't move. She was in an untenable predicament. He was an expert lover—gentle, sensitive to her desires. Their bodies came together perfectly. But there should be more. It was useless to deny that his hands, his lips, his husky voice sent her into a mindless whirl of pleasure. She shivered, his arms tightened, and she wept silently.

"I can't get enough of you," he whispered as his lips traced a path across her forehead. He grasped her hand and held it palm down against the flat plain of his stomach. Her whole body went rigid as she fought the tremors of longing that were already shaking her control. She stifled the sob that rose in her throat and resisted surrender when his mouth came to rest on hers. His probing tongue encountered sealed lips where minutes ago it had found eager admittance. His hands became more demanding, his lips more persuasive, and she parted her own lips to object, to protest that she didn't want him again. He used that instant to find what he was seeking, and the touch of his tongue on her threatened to rob her of the ability to think, to remember the cold-eyed man who had treated her scornfully in Boston.

No! her pride screamed. He didn't love her. He was using her to satisfy his sexual lust. Her body shook with a different kind of tremor that Jonathan responded to immediately. He lifted his mouth and she buried her face against the damp, matted hair on his chest. Tenderly his fingers raised her face and moved over her cheeks, wet with tears.

"Don't make love to me again. Please . . . I don't want you to," she stammered.

"All right, sweetheart. But were my caresses so terrible?" His voice was soft and persuasive. "You enjoyed it, didn't you?" His lips were moving over her face, absorbing her tears. "I know I did."

"I don't want to get pregnant," she blurted out. "I would hate it!"

He remained still for a long while, raining gentle kisses on her face and holding her very tightly.

"Are you sure, Kelly? Are you sure you don't want us to have a child?" he whispered in her ear, and kissed her so gently that her whole body cried out for him.

She raised tear-drenched lashes that fluttered against his cheek. A wave of helplessness came over her, and she whimpered. As if in torment, she tightened her arms about his neck and hungrily sought his lips, wanting to escape her anguished thoughts. He remained perfectly still as her mouth moved over his.

"This is all we have," she sobbed helplessly. "I despise your snobbish way of life and you'll hate mine after you've tried it. It would be criminal for us to have a child. No! I never want to have a child by you, Jonathan!"

Her words made him go rigid. "If you're sure, Kelly," he said slowly. "If you're very sure you never want to have my child, I'll go to Anchorage and have a vasectomy."

His words stunned her. Had he really said them? He would give up, forever, the chance to have a child of his own?

"No!" Her arms clutched him frantically and her hands moved over his powerful body. "No! I couldn't let you do that. Oh, Jonathan, what are we going to do?"

His arms pulled her closer as her tears wet his chest. He rained kisses on her brow, cheeks, and throat. Her own mouth blindly sought comfort, tasting her salty tears on his lips, and the tang of his skin. The driving force of her passion was taking her beyond reason, beyond fear.

"Don't think about it, darling. If you don't want

a baby, we'll do something about it. But for now
. . . we'll have to take the risk, because I can't
stop. . . ."

She sighed deeply and then blocked out everything but this moment . . . this night. She heard his
ragged breathing as if from far away, and then she
pulled him to her. Gradually the storm of passion
overpowered them and they made wild, uninhib-
ited love.

Afterward she lay quietly beside him. He
buried his face in the curve of her neck, like a
child seeking comfort. She held him and stroked
him without speaking. But she couldn't dismiss a
feeling of impending doom. Her need for him
was making her a prisoner and inwardly she
rebelled.

"I could have you again," he whispered hoarsely
against her breast.

Kelly's mouth went dry. "Again?"

He laughed and nibbled her skin. "It's been a
long, dry spell."

"Am I supposed to believe that?" she asked quietly.

"Absolutely," he said firmly and caught the lobe
of her ear with his teeth and nipped it before
burying his face in the hollow between her
breasts. "Has there ever been another man?" he
muttered. "Don't lie to me. Just tell me if you've
slept with another man."

"There's been no other man."

He lifted his head and covered her mouth with his, and for a long time there was only the sound of their shaken breathing and the thump of his heart pounding against hers.

"Thank you, darling," he said in a voice trembling with emotion. "I had to hear you say you've been only mine."

Something hurt inside her. She swallowed convulsively. He wanted to own her, possess her for his pleasure alone. What happened tonight would happen again and again. What had she expected? a small voice cried inside her. She and Jonathan couldn't live in the same house, much less sleep in the same bed without sex. It all boiled down to one thing: an arrangement. She would give Jonathan the sex he wanted and he, in turn, would let Mike and Marty keep the resort. It was as cold-blooded as that.

She had to sort out her emotions, untangle the confused motivations, and decide what she really wanted out of life. The image of Jack she had carried in her heart for so long had surfaced. The cold, possessive Jonathan of Boston had faded to nothingness when Jack held her in his arms. She needed time to think. She had rushed into marriage without any real idea of the kind of man she was marrying or the kind of lifestyle she would be expected to live. She couldn't afford to make that mistake again. If her home in Alaska was a prison, at least it wasn't the kind of prison Boston had been, where everything pressed down on her, chilling her, crushing her spirit.

Jonathan's hand slowly stroked her back. "What are you thinking about?"

"Our Boston apartment and what a beautiful prison it was."

He drew in a long, shaken breath and stroked the hair from her temples, his fingers touching her cheeks.

"And I was the warden? What do you feel for me, Kelly?" he asked wearily.

She moved her hand to his chest and felt his heart leaping under it. The rest of him was still, with a peculiar, silent waiting between them.

"Feelings shouldn't be involved where business is concerned, Jonathan," she whispered in husky tones.

He turned on his back and drew her to him. She settled her head on his body and heard the slow, regular rhythm of his breathing. His hands touched her gently, without pressure, as though reassuring himself she was here.

"Are you warm?" he asked and tucked the blankets close behind her.

"Uh-huh."

Finally she fell asleep.

CHAPTER EIGHT

SHE REFUSED TO open her eyes. She wanted to fall asleep again, because in sleep there was no regret, no incrimination.

"Kelly!" Her name was a soft whisper wooing her from the land of Nod. She turned her face into the pillow and the insistent voice grew crisper. "Kelly!"

"What do you want?" she said crossly into the pillow.

"It's nine o'clock."

"Nine o'clock?" Her eyes flew open and she turned to glance up at Jonathan standing beside the bed with a mug in his hand. "Nine o'clock? I don't believe it!"

"You've been sleeping like a baby for hours." He sat down on the bed. He had shaved, his hair was damp from the shower, and he was fully dressed in clean denims and a soft flannel shirt. "Drink your coffee and come alive, woman."

Kelly freed her arms from the confines of the soft, fleecy blanket and pushed her tangled hair back from her sleep-flushed face. She looked into teasing, brown eyes and was flooded with the sudden memory of the ecstasy she had shared with him just hours before. Shame and humiliation made her voice sharp.

"Nothing is changed!"

114

"What do you mean?" He handed her the mug which she was forced to take.

"You know what I mean. You seduced me, wore me down. I'll never forgive you!"

"Kelly, Kelly . . . I'm not asking for your forgiveness. All I did was make love to my wife, a normal, healthy expression of emotion."

The calm inflection in his quiet voice grated on her nerves and resentment burned in her eyes.

"Expression of emotion? Lust, you mean!"

"Lust or a biological urge. I prefer to think of it as making love." He smiled at her warmly.

"Love had nothing to do with it!" She spat the words at him and jerked the blanket up to her chin.

He laughed and she wanted to hit him. "Okay. Call it anything you want . . . but I liked doing it!"

"I don't give a damn what you call it! It won't happen again. I won't be a . . . a vehicle for your lust!" The words exploded from her tense lips.

"My lust? Our lust, dear wife. Or is lust too masculine a word to describe a woman's sexual desires?" Amusement glinted in his dark eyes.

"Sex? Lust? Is that all you can talk about?"

Heavy lids hid his eyes and a secretive smile curved his mouth. Bending forward, he brushed his lips tantalizingly across hers. "Let's not fight, Kelly. Let's make love."

With a groan of irritation, she turned away from him. "I wish you hadn't come here!" she said viciously.

"You'll get over it. After I've been here a few weeks, you'll wonder how you ever lived without me." He took the mug from her hand and set it on the bedside table, then rubbed his fingers back and forth across her cheek. "We'll discuss this tonight while we're lying together in this bed, our arms around each other. It's good, isn't it? This touching and feeling every part of each other? We make love well, darling."

Kelly wanted to jerk away, but pride forced her to pretend his touch didn't bother her. She remained perfectly still, although her heart pounded like a scared rabbit's, and she kept her eyes averted. With a quick movement he flicked aside the blanket to reveal her long, slender, naked figure.

"Stop that!" She grabbed for the blanket.

He laughed and went around the end of the bed toward the door. "I'm expecting a chopper in about fifteen minutes. One of my men is bringing in some paperwork. I thought I would do the work in the chopper. Do you think you can get along without me for an hour or so?"

"Try me."

He grinned broadly. "I'll send the chopper away if you think you'll die of lust before I can get back." The amusement on his face enraged her. She clamped her lips together and refused to speak the words that boiled up in her. "The water is hot for your shower. Leave the water tank turned on. We can afford to have hot water all day."

"Sure. Now that Mountain View is part of a big conglomerate, we're merely a tax write-off." The reminder that her home was no longer hers tore at her heart.

"Think what you like, Kelly." He drawled her name. "There are times when you tempt me to swat your behind."

Across the room her eyes challenged him and her thoughts whirled. If she stayed another night with him . . . if she slept another night in his arms. . . . Oh, she had to hold out against him!

"You're not staying here!" she almost shouted at him, but he had already left the room.

On her way to the lodge, Kelly paused to play with Charlie for a few minutes. Mike's utility truck was parked in the shed and a plume of smoke came from his cabin chimney. For one wild instant Kelly was tempted to go there and tell him what Jonathan had done. There was no doubt in her mind that Mike would agree to go away with her and leave the property to Jonathan. But she couldn't do that to Mike. He would expect her to divorce Jonathan and marry him. Head down and hands buried deep in the pockets of her coat, she headed toward the lodge, her mind so busy she failed to see the tall doctor waiting beside the steps.

"You look as gorgeous today as you did yesterday."

Kelly looked up into his smiling eyes. "Hi, Andy.

Bye, Andy. I'm headed for the kitchen and gallons of coffee."

He slipped his hand beneath her elbow and they went up the steps together. "I had breakfast with your husband. He said you were tired and sleeping in."

The statement required no answer and Kelly shrugged out of her jacket and slipped off her boots. She could like Andy, if only Jonathan hadn't come to the resort and stirred up all the emotions she had thought dead. If only Jonathan was more like Andy . . . Kelly put a brake on her thoughts. She could *if only* until doomsday and it wouldn't change a thing.

"Come out, come out, from wherever you are!" Andy bent down and grinned into her face. "Back among the living? Do you suppose that husband of yours would let you take a snowmobile ride with me?"

"What's it got to do with him? How about askin' me, buster?" Although Kelly's tone was teasing, he held an underlying note of seriousness.

"Okay." He placed his hand over his heart. "Andy Mullins respectfully requests the honor of your presence . . ."

"Oh, stop!" Kelly laughed. "I'd love to go, but first I need to fortify myself with some of Bonnie's toast and coffee." She led the way into the kitchen. "What about your friends? Would they like to go, too? We can carry four."

"They're busy resting, sleeping in. I wouldn't be surprised if it took all day for them to rest up." His eyes twinkled down at her. She ignored the implication.

"If you say so. Morning, Bonnie." She took a cup from the rack. "Coffee, Andy?"

"Sure. A roll, too. I've already asked Bonnie to divorce Clyde and marry me. She's not only beautiful, she's also got the fastest cookstove in the West!"

"You ain't gonna eat again!" Bonnie put her hands on her ample hips, tried to look disgusted, and failed completely.

"Now, darlin', you said, and I quote: 'Ain't nothin' does my heart so good as to see a man what likes his vittles.' You said that not an hour ago." Andy took the cup Kelly handed him and sat down at the table. "All I want is one little ol' roll."

"You don't have to pay no attention to everything I say! You'll spoil your dinner, that's what you'll do," Bonnie scolded. "I'm having Irish stew for dinner and barbecue ribs for supper. Clyde's already got them in the smoker."

"I promise to eat my share. Now hand over that roll before I shoot up the place." He shaped his hand like a six-gun and pointed it at her.

"I swear to goodness, Kelly," Bonnie complained. "I thought Jack could eat a lot, but this kid can outdo even him. I think we ought to add another twenty bucks to his bill."

"Good idea." Kelly lifted the bread from the toaster and sat down across from Andy. "Some kid!" she said softly for his ears alone.

"Jack had a stack of hot cakes and three pats of sausage this morning," Bonnie volunteered. She set down in front of Andy a roll as big as a saucer, dripping with melted butter, and glazed with icing. "He said a friend was coming in a helicopter to bring him some things and to make a list if I wanted anything. I said, well, we sure could use a new washer and dryer cause the ones we got must have come with the gold-rushers." Kelly looked up sharply and Bonnie, catching the disapproval on her face, added quickly, "I was just a teasin'. I didn't put nothing like that on the list. I wrote down some things like spices and a couple cases of tomatoes and a new broom. I wanted to add towels, but thought that better wait till one of us can go to the discount store. Men ain't got no sense a'tall when it comes to a buyin' something like that." She went back to the stove and lifted the lid on a large cooking pot. The grin she shot over her shoulder held just a dash of superiority. "Smell that, Andy? That stew's goin' to be just right!"

Kelly drove the snowmobile and Andy sat in the seat behind her. Her spirits picked up when they headed for open country. The snow was light and the churning lugs of the machine left a soft, fine cloud behind them. They followed animal tracks just to see where they were going and once Kelly stopped the machine when she saw a small herd of moose move out of the timber.

"You can never tell what a moose will do," she explained to Andy. "If pointed in your direction, they might run right over you. They get confused and sometimes jump out in front of cars. It happened to Mike and me once. We saw the moose coming and there was nothing we could do. Mike shoved me down on the seat and boom! We had a moose draped over the hood. The windshield popped out and we almost froze, driving in below-zero weather without a windshield."

Andy was a pleasant companion. Kelly showed him wolf tracks and told him that the legend about the wolf being a vicious killer was a myth.

"My father always thought the wolf was a very misunderstood animal. He kills only to eat, and rarely attacks man. He is a lonely animal. Occasionally, on a clear night we can hear his mournful howl. A wolverine is an altogether different and much more dangerous animal." Kelly shuddered.

As they drove back to the lodge, the breeze rushing against Kelly's face and the snow whipping about her cleared her head and soothed her taut nerves. She had deliberately stayed away from the helicopter, which sat like a large insect on the white snow.

In the deserted family room of the lodge they sank down onto the couch and Andy told her about his job on the reservation. A soft light came into his eyes as he talked. He was dedicated to his work among the Indians. He told her of their pride, their dignity, and their great need. Andy was a fine man, she decided.

"Have you ever been married?" she asked suddenly.

"Sure," he laughed. "Hasn't everyone?"

"Divorced?" She didn't know why she persisted.

"Ages ago. She's married to a banker now. Couldn't stand my lifestyle. Nothing prestigious about living in a five room bungalow on an Indian reservation." All traces of merriment were gone from his face.

"She and Jonathan would have been great together." The words came before Kelly realized she was saying them.

"Now, now," Andy chided gently. "Methinks you . . ."

" Kelly was saved from hearing more by Bonnie entering through the swinging doors.

"Dinner is ready anytime anybody wants to eat it."

Kelly's laughing eyes caught Andy's. "We're very informal here, or hadn't you noticed?"

"Is that what it is?" Andy asked innocently. "I like it. Reserve me a room for the last weekend of the month. I'm attending a seminar in Anchorage or I wouldn't leave here at all."

"Landsakes! I'll start a cookin' on a Thursday if I know he's comin' on the weekend. I'll have to get me a runnin' start to fill him up!" Bonnie's face was a wreath of smiles even as she complained.

"Marty and Tram will be here by then. Maybe we can plan an overnight ski-tour."

"Overnight?" Andy frowned, then grinned. "Dibs on sharing my sleeping bag with you."

"You're nuts! Do you know that?"

"Jack would have something to say about that," Bonnie said. She cocked her head and listened. "That's the chopper leavin'. Jack ought to be up here in a few minutes."

He was.

The instant he stepped inside the door, his eyes locked with Kelly's and she felt a pain deep inside her. Their hours of making love had pried open the dark door between them and brought her face to face with the Jack behind the sophisticated facade of Jonathan Templeton the Third.

Jonathan left his coat and boots beside the door and went directly to Kelly, pulling her up from the couch.

"Enjoy your ride, darling?" His arm went possessively across her shoulders.

"How did you know?"

He chuckled and his arm tightened. "How could I miss that yellow cap of yours?"

"True," she murmured drily.

"What we need is a good bit of that stew."

Bonnie seemed to sense the tension and burst into speech. "I'll just step out on the back step and holler to that ugly old Clyde. He's out there a tinkerin' with that old motor again. Yaw'll go on in . . . everything's ready. I'll be right along and dip up the stew."

They had scarcely reached the kitchen when they heard Bonnie scream.

Kelly dashed for the back door, but Jonathan was there ahead of her. Bonnie lay in a heap at the foot of the steps, her leg twisted under her and her back against the rise of the stairs. They could see the path her feet had made when she slipped on the loose snow covering the icy platform at the top of the steps.

Andy was beside her in an instant. "Don't move. Lie still, Bonnie. Let me see what you've done to yourself."

Clyde came running from the shed. "What did you do, honeybunch? I told ya to be careful on that ice. Are ya hurt?"

Bonnie looked dazed. Her face and hair were wet with snow. "Clyde! Clyde, honey, I hurt my back . . . and my leg . . . 'n', oh, hell, I hurt all over!" Her face twisted with pain and her lips quivered.

Andy's experienced hands were traveling over her leg.

"Get a blanket, Kelly," he said without looking up. Gentle fingers lifted Bonnie's chin. "For one thing, you've gone and busted yore leg and I'll have to shoot ya!" he said in a perfect imitation of her Oklahoma twang. To Clyde he said, "We need a flat board. She may have injured her back."

"There's a piece of plywood in the shed." Clyde began to rise to his feet, but Jonathan put his hand on his shoulder.

"I'll get it. Stay with Bonnie."

Kelly held the door open while the men carried Bonnie into the kitchen. She was obviously in great pain and tears seeped from her eyes, leaving dark streaks of mascara on her cheeks.

"I've really gone and done it, ain't I, Clyde? We had a good place here . . . oh, I'm so sorry, honey. I ruined everything!"

"Now you quit frettin'. You didn't do it on purpose. We'll get by. Ain't we always managed?"

Clyde tried to calm Bonnie while Kelly went for more blankets and Andy got his medical kit.

"How are we going to pay for this, Clyde? We ain't got no insurance." Bonnie began to cry in earnest.

"The lodge will pay the bills, Bonnie," Jonathan reassured her. "Don't worry. All you've got to do is lie still until we can get you out of here." Jonathan stood beside the table where they had set the board with Bonnie still on it.

"They can't, Jack! Them kids scraped up every penny they could. They worked so hard to get this place going. They was so good to me and Clyde. It'll break 'em if they got big bills and . . ."

"Insurance will pay it. Stop worrying."

"They ain't got no insurance. Kelly told us . . ."

"They have. I took care of it. Now, Clyde, see if you can get Mike up here so he can get on that radio. I'm sure he knows more about reaching the helicopter that just left here than I do."

Kelly helped Andy prepare Bonnie for the trip and Jonathan sat down at the table and quickly filled a sheet of paper with his strong handwriting. With the use of an emergency relay system, Mike was able to get a message to the helicopter pilot with orders to turn back to the resort.

An hour later they carried a sedated Bonnie, bundled in wool blankets, out to the clearing. Jonathan spoke to the pilot while Mike, Andy, and Clyde maneuvered the stretcher into place.

The three men stood back, as the powerful blades whipped the soft snow into a cloud, and waited for the helicopter to lift off. Afterward, they crowded into the cab of the truck and, with Mike driving, went back to the lodge.

CHAPTER NINE

"You'll do no such thing!" Kelly's hands were deep in sudsy dishwater and she flung the words over her shoulder. They'd just served late lunch and she was in the midst of cleaning up. "Bring a chef out here! What do you think this is, the Mountain View Hilton?"

"You can't do all your usual work and the cooking, too, Kelly." Jonathan's calm voice grated on her already taut nerves.

"What makes you think I can't? I'm no delicate social butterfly, Jonathan. Butt out, will you? Marty will be here next week and we'll manage just fine."

He took a deep breath. His face was a dark mask and his voice was harsh.

"One of these days you're going to push me too far and I'm going to take a strap to your butt!"

She turned in surprise to see his eyes flickering over her face and his nostrils flaring.

"Ha!" she exploded. "I can see the headlines . . . 'Member Of Boston's Social Register Turns Wife Beater.'"

Jonathan suddenly looked so furious that all the strength drained out of her, leaving her limp in the grip of the hands that shook her.

"I'm tired of your ridicule! If you make one more derogatory reference to my background, I'm going to shake you until your teeth rattle!"

Kelly gazed into his eyes, so astonishingly bright with anger. "And what would that prove?" she demanded. "That you're bigger and stronger than I am? You want to hurt me, so go ahead!"

"You're damn right I want to hurt you! Don't you know you hurt me by walking out on me and letting me worry half to death over you?"

"The only thing I ever hurt was your pride. My rejection was a blow to your ego." She spit the words out recklessly and trembled with unspent emotion. "I was doing very well until you came. This is my home, where I belong. You'll never get me away from here, Jonathan, even if our property is in your name. You still don't own the business, so don't tell me how to run it."

His gaze was locked with hers, as her voice lashed him with bitter, unguarded words. "Don't make me lose my temper, Kelly," he said softly.

"You can't take my life over and dictate what I'll do."

"I'm not trying to take over your life. I'm trying to share it."

"Then let me go so I can wipe the dishes."

His hand slid along her spine, pulling her close to him. His eyes teased her. "Ask me nicely and I will."

"You're the most changeable, obstinate man I've ever known."

"Determined," he corrected softly.

"Obstinate, stubborn, mulish, pigheaded . . . stiff-necked!"

"At least you'll never be bored with me." He brushed her mouth with his lips.

"And I'll never have a moment of peace, either."

He lifted her chin, tilting her head up to stare down into her eyes. She tried to pull away, and her hair brushed his face. His eyes narrowed with desire.

The intensity of his gaze made her uncomfortable but she returned his look coolly. "What you see is what you get." She regretted the words immediately.

His grin spread a terrible charm over his face and she felt a smile touch her own. She tried to banish it.

"Is that a promise?" He placed a feathery kiss on her nose.

"You're maddening!" She snapped her teeth at him.

"And you're not?" He took her hand and she felt something hard against her fingers. Looking down, she saw the blue flash of a sapphire. He slipped the plain wedding band onto her finger and then the sapphire and diamond ring. He folded her fingers into her palm and held them there. "It's time these were back where they belong."

She sucked in her breath, dismayed. Before she could say a word he bent his head and kissed her gently. Tides of overwhelming warmth washed over her.

"I've got to get these dishes done." She had to get away from him. The ache in her body was too much to bear. She had to keep busy.

"And I'd better fill the woodbox. That was one of Clyde's jobs, wasn't it?"

"That and keeping the fires going, the ashes hauled out, the wood cut, etc., etc., etc. . . . ."

"Keeping the heat tapes on the pipes, checking

the well pump, keeping the motors going, necking with the cook, etc., etc., etc. . . ." He grinned. "You think I can't manage a few simple chores?"

"Seein' is believin'." She turned her back to him and plunged her hands into the dishwater.

"Some of those chores can wait until I wipe a few dishes."

They worked silently side by side. Kelly's hands moved automatically while her mind strived to sort out Jonathan's confusing behavior. It would be wishful thinking to believe he felt more than pure desire for her. His determination to stay with her arose from simple frustration. A spoiled little boy had grown into a hard, sophisticated man who had been denied something he wanted very badly.

Once she had given him her love, and he had dropped it carelessly. Now, he wanted back the toy that had been snatched away from him. In his determination to possess her, he was robbing her of any chance to forget him, any chance for finding happiness with someone new.

She finished the last dish and straightened her aching back. "You're tired, you silly girl. Sit down and have a cup of coffee." Jonathan pushed her gently into a chair. "I'll see about the ribs in the smoker and fill the cookstove before I check the fireplace and take a run down to our house to be sure it's warm enough there."

"All right, Dangerous Dan McGrew," she said without humor.

"If I'm Dan McGrew, you're the lady that's known as Lou," he said softly.

"Don't tell me Yukon poetry was included in the curriculum at your fancy boarding school."

Jonathan stood before her, his expression serious, and began reciting:

"There are strange things done in the midnight sun
    By men who moil for gold;
The Arctic trails have their secret tales
    That would make your blood run cold;
The Northern Lights have seen queer sights,
    But the queerest they ever did see
Was the night on the marge of Lake Lebarge
    I cremated Sam McGee.

That, my darling wife, is from a poem by Robert Service, poet of the Yukon, who worked in a Whitehorse bank that's still doing business."

"Hear! Hear!" Kelly cheered, a big grin on her face. She loved poetry, especially ballads. "We'll work up a floor show and let you entertain the guests," she teased.

"And run the risk of losing me to Las Vegas?"

"I wouldn't be so lucky." There was no sting in her tone; her eyes were still warm with laughter.

"No appreciation. That's what's wrong with you, my girl." She watched him put his coat on and thought how easy it would be to fall back into the trap of blind adoration, accepting the desire he offered as a substitute for the love she craved. "Don't go away," he said lightly.

Preparations for the evening meal went smoothly. The food Bonnie had cooked that morning helped ease the workload, and Jonathan proved to be far more capable than Kelly had imagined. He scrubbed and oiled the potatoes, while she prepared greens for the salad. Finally, she couldn't supress a giggle.

"What's funny?" he asked.

"You'd know if you could see yourself. I never expected to see the perfectly groomed, cool, no-nonsense Jonathan Templeton with soot on his face." She began to laugh. "You don't look very elegant."

He laughed too. "*You* look elegant!" He grabbed a stack of plates. "What's the program? Do we all eat together?"

"I'll be waitress. Set places for the five guests and yourself."

"I'll be waiter. We can eat together afterward. How about Mike?"

"He said he'd be up later."

"When did he say that?"

"While we were waiting for the helicopter to come for Bonnie." She glanced around the kitchen and dining area. It looked neat and cozy. With the exception of the potatoes baking in the oven, the meal was ready to be served. She whipped off her apron, and took a large tray from the shelf.

"Now what?" Jonathan asked.

"Drinks. I think we should serve before-dinner drinks."

"Good idea. That's my department. Move aside and let the bartender take over." He loaded the tray with glasses, mix, whiskey, and rum. Kelly filled a bowl with ice cubes and reached for cocktail napkins. Jonathan looked over the tray with a critical eye then, with a conspiratorial wink, he headed for the swinging doors.

He was a perfect host. Why not, Kelly thought. He'd certainly had enough practice. As the murmur of amused chatter flowed over her, Kelly experienced a feeling of unreality. It was almost as if she and Jonathan were entertaining guests in their own home.

While she served the meal, Jonathan set two places at a small table at the far end of the room. He smiled a lot in a slow, endearing way that lifted his mouth at the corners and spread a warm light into his eyes. She hadn't seen him smile like that since . . . Anchorage.

Kelly bantered pleasantly with Andy. The girl who had been so attentive to Jonathan the night before seemed to have transfered her attention to Andy tonight. Her nonstop chatter didn't leave room for much other conversation.

Jonathan and Kelly were silent during their own meal. When they'd finished, Jonathan carried their empty plates to the sink.

"Charlie will love the rib bones," he said, returning with the coffee pot. It was cozy and quiet and music from the stereo drifted softly into the room. "It went off without a hitch, didn't it?" He had a satisfied smile on his face.

"Yes, it did," she admitted.

The back door opened and Mike entered. "Smells good," he said. "Anything left?"

"Sure. Help yourself." Suddenly the room felt cold. Jonathan leaned back in his chair, maddeningly in command of himself. A look flashed between them. Don't freeze Mike out of my life! Kelly's mind shrieked. Her eyes shifted to Mike and she smiled. "Fill a plate and join us."

Jonathan was watching her shrewdly, eyes narrowed, as he sipped his coffee. Kelly didn't know what to expect next.

"Bring a cup, Mike. The coffee pot is here," he said, his eyes still on Kelly.

"The potatoes are in the warming oven," she added.

"All this and potatoes, too? I'm hungry as a bear."

They spoke polite words, but might as well have snarled at each other. Kelly was surprised at how confidently Mike approached them, and felt a flash of pride. He was family and she loved him. She was sure that one day soon he would realize he loved her like family, too. Her eyes softened when she looked at him.

"You'll have to clue me in on what's to be done around here while Clyde's away, Mike," Jonathan said easily.

"Think you can handle Clyde's chores? I can always get a few no-good loafers to come out for a while. I would have done that before, but I wouldn't leave Kelly out here alone with most of them."

Kelly met Jonathan's eyes with a pretense of calm. Mike was handling himself just fine.

"I appreciate that."

Kelly flushed. Those three words set his seal of possession on her.

"If you think you can manage it, we'd better get on the ends of that crosscut in the morning. I cut enough wood this fall for my own use, but I didn't know Kelly was coming back or that she'd want to open the lodge. Heat is top priority in this country."

"Have you looked into propane gas for heating?" Jonathan asked.

"Can't afford it. It would cost an arm and a leg to heat this place with gas. Maybe later when we get the business going."

Here it comes, Kelly thought. Jonathan would reveal that he owned the lodge and Mike would be furious! She felt caught between two hungry dogs.

"I've been thinking" she interrupted anxiously. "Now that hunting season is on and the moose are coming down out of the timber, we could hire someone to butcher the animals our guests shoot. It might be an added incentive to bring hunters to the lodge. They could take the meat home in neat packages instead of draped over the top of the car."

"You should be banned from thinking, wooden-head," Mike said affectionately. "How many hunters would drive out here? If they come at all, it will be by train. Besides, they'll want to take their prize back and show it off before it's butchered. We've got the truck to haul it to the sta-tion. Anyway, if we set up that kind of operation, we'd have a hundred inspectors out here with a thousand different regulations."

"He's right, sweetheart," Jonathan said. "It's out of the question."

Jonathan and Mike were agreeing on some-thing—and against her! She wanted to be angry, but instead felt relief. "Well, if that's the way you feel about it . . ." She gave them both a mocking smile and got up from the table. "I'll take my ideas to the dishpan. That's one idea you'll both approve of, I'm sure." Both men laughed and sud-denly Kelly was almost happy.

"I'll help you." Jonathan began to clear the table. "About tonight, Mike. What do you suggest we do about . . ."

"I'll stay in the lodge tonight," he said quickly. "I can't do much to fill in for Clyde, but I can stay up here nights."

"Do we have to socialize with the guests?" Jonathan asked when he brought a load of dishes to the sink.

"I can do that, too," Mike said with a grin. "There's a cute little blonde in there who's been giving me the eye."

Kelly could scarcely believe the evening had ended so pleasantly. The weather was cold, hovering around the zero mark, when she and Jonathan walked down the snow-packed path to her cabin. Charlie came bounding out to meet them, the ever present, battered frisbee in his mouth. He headed straight for Jonathan.

Later, when Jonathan lifted the blankets, slid into bed beside her, and took her flannel-gowned body in his arms, she made no protest. She was so tired. She snuggled against his warm body and was asleep almost instantly.

CHAPTER TEN

MARTY AND TRAM arrived with the announcement that they had been married the day before in Fairbanks.

"We decided we didn't need that little piece of paper to stay together," Marty explained. "Then as long as we didn't need it, we thought we might as well get it."

Mike glowered at his sister, yanked a box out of the utility truck, and carried it to the cabin where she and her new husband would live. Tram had already disappeared inside and Jonathan was at the lodge.

"It's a shock to Mike that you're all grown up," Kelly explained with a laugh.

"Gripes! I don't know why it should be. We're the same age. All three of us, as a matter of fact. The best thing for him would be to find himself a woman!" Marty picked up one of the suitcases and reached for a smaller one. "Let's leave the rest of this for Tram and get in out of the cold."

Tram was a tall, thin man of thirty. His hair was thick and curly, a warm, golden toffee color. He was attractive in an unconventional way. The sudden smile that came over his face when he looked at Marty plainly said he adored her, which endeared him to Kelly immediately.

"Mike said your husband is here. Is he going to stay?" Marty shrugged out of her coat and dumped it on a chair. She was a slender girl with full breasts and narrow hips. She raised her straight brows and her wide mouth tilted into a grin. "I'm anxious to meet the fabulous Jonathan Templeton. I saw his picture in *Newsweek* a couple of months ago."

"What was that all about?" Kelly asked quietly.

"He resigned as chairman of the board of some big company and turned over the management of several other companies. I don't know anything about business, but it was something like that. The stock market did something or other when that happened." She looked closely at Kelly. "What's a man like him doing here? Are you going back to him?"

"I'm not going back *with* him, if that's what you mean. And as to what he's doing here, he says he's going to stay and help us run the resort." Kelly's voice dropped on the last word and Marty shook her head sadly.

"Are you still in love with him?" When Kelly didn't answer, she said, "You are! Well then, what's the problem?"

"I don't know if I love him or not. Sometimes I think I do and other times I know I don't. We don't fit, that's the crux of the whole thing. I was out of my depth, Marty. The months I spent in Boston were the most miserable of my life. I can't explain it. I was a different person there and so was the man I married. I was afraid to move in case I did something wrong. His friends made it clear I was an intruder. His sister despised me. And he became cold and remote. It was awful!"

"How is he now?"

"At first he was belligerent. Now he seems more relaxed and at times I think he enjoys himself."

"Do you sleep with him?" Marty asked bluntly.

Kelly's tongue moistened her lips. "Yes, I do."

Marty's blue eyes grew warm. "You crazy girl! I know you wouldn't sleep with him unless you cared for him!"

"Jonathan isn't an easy man to refuse." Kelly lifted stricken eyes.

Marty whistled. "Hell's bells!"

"Did you whistle for me, lover?" Tram came in and planted a kiss on Marty's mouth.

"Would you come running if I did?"

"Try me," he said, and pinched her bottom.

"Did Mike leave?" Kelly asked.

"Just a minute ago." Tram sat down to take off his boots and Marty hung up his coat.

"The blockhead! Now I'll have to walk up to the lodge. You two come on up around six-thirty and we'll have a before-dinner drink. I made a special dinner for your homecoming, if Jonathan hasn't let the fire go out in the cookstove." Kelly pulled her yellow wool hat down over her ears and wound her red scarf about her neck. "I'll leave you lovebirds alone."

Out in the crisp cold she walked with head down toward the lodge. She felt rather depressed about her own situation, but happy for Marty. Marty deserved to be happy. If only she and Tram and Mike could stay here. If only Jonathan hadn't paid those taxes . . . There she went again, she chided herself. Instead of worrying about the *if onlys,* she should be concerned about the *what ifs.* What if Jonathan told them he was the man in charge here? What if he made Marty feel unwelcome?

Jonathan did neither. He was relaxed, friendly,

charming, helpful, and made it blatantly clear that he and Kelly were a team.

"I like him," Marty said while she and Kelly were cleaning the kitchen. "I can see him as the big business executive, though. He's very possessive of you, isn't he? He could scarcely keep his hands off you. I think he's head over heels in love with you."

"You're right about everything up to that point." Kelly lifted a big bone out of the roasting pan for Charlie. "It wounded his pride when I left him, but love me? . . . He doesn't! He hasn't mentioned a word about love. It's want, want, want, and you're mine. I won't be used that way!"

Marty looked at her for a long time before she said, "I wish I had some earth-shaking words of wisdom for you. The only thing I can say is to hang in there. He may change, but I wouldn't count on it."

"Count on what?" Her twin came up behind her.

"None of your business, brother. If you're going to butt in, grab a towel."

"That's woman's work!" He put an arm around each girl. "Never thought I'd get both of my girls back to take care of me. I've got the biggest washing, and . . ."

"Chauvinist! Get your own woman!" Marty kissed him on the cheek.

"Good idea. This one's spoken for," Jonathan said from behind Kelly. His arm went about her waist and he pulled her back against him.

"Ah . . . ha!" Marty cried. "You've lost out again, brother. You should have let me fix you up with Geraldine Jenkins. She can cook fabulous meals, sew, make jerky, tan hides . . ."

"But she's fat!"

"So? She can go on a diet come spring."

"By spring she couldn't get through that door!"

"Complain, complain, complain! Never satisfied, is he, Kelly? Tram! Tram, darling. Come take this brother away and tell him about the birds and the bees so Kelly and I can get this mess cleared away."

Pulled tightly back against Jonathan, Kelly listened to the light banter between these two people she loved so much. Her husband's warm breath tickled her ear and his heart thudded against her back. If only he could see Mike and Marty as she did. Why did she have to feel so pulled between him and them?

"Do you want help?" Jonathan asked against her ear. She turned her head slightly and warm lips found the corner of her mouth.

"There isn't that much to do. Marty and I'll do it."

Jonathan removed his arm after a brief squeeze. "Come on, Mike. I know it's a mind-blowing thought, but I don't think they appreciate us."

"Before you go, take this pan out for Charlie." Kelly held out the deep pan filled with table scraps.

His smile was charming, endearing, and Kelly's heart did a flip. Jack! Damn . . . she had to stop thinking about Jack.

"Charlie will appreciate me," Jonathan grumbled and headed for the door.

Minutes later, Kelly and Marty joined the men before a huge fire in the family room. Jonathan was reclining on a bearskin rug with his back to an ottoman and pulled Kelly down beside him. She curled her feet up under her.

"Feet cold? Hold them close to the fire. It's below zero out there." His arm tightened around her. Just another way to let everyone else know I belong to him, Kelly thought drily.

"What do you think, Mike?" Tram took up the conversation. "Do we have a level enough space over in that clearing to launch a glider?"

"A glider?" Marty echoed. "You don't know anything about gliding."

"That's what you think, oh sweet one. I've had an ache to try my hand at gliding for a long time. Jack's got a motorized glider."

"Sounds dangerous," Marty protested.

"It really isn't, Marty," Jonathan said. "When I was in Iowa last summer I tried it and got hooked. The young fellow who builds them taught me how to fly in just a few days. You sit under the wing in a harness suspended from the frame. A control bar in front of the harness connects to the rudder with control lines. The pilot controls the glider by shifting his weight. Lean back and it climbs; lean forward and it dives; move to the right, the glider turns right."

"Still sounds dangerous. How high up do you go? Tram, I'd die of fright if you flew in such a thing!"

Jonathan laughed, and tightened his arm around Kelly. "How about you, honey? Would it frighten you?"

"Depends. It sounds fragile."

"It is. It's only a hundred and fifty pounds of Dacron and aluminum powered by a fifteen-horse, two-cylinder motor. I figure we could put skis on it and pull it with the snowmobile to get it started. Think that would work, Mike?"

"It will if twenty-five miles an hour will get you airborne." Mike's eyes shone with interest.

"That should do it. The contraption is still packed in crates. You fellows will have to help me assemble it." Jonathan laughed. "Mechanics is not my long suit."

"We can put it together if we have the instructions." Mike's blue eyes were now dancing with enthusiasm.

"I still think you're crazy," Marty said. "It'll be too damn cold to work on the thing until spring."

"We can work in the shed," Mike said. "We've got an old potbellied wood stove I can set up. It will be warm enough for us to work."

"I knew it," Marty groaned. "Just mention putting a model together and he's off like a shot. Remember, Kelly, when he spent hours and hours on his darned old models and wouldn't play with us?" She put her hand on the top of Tram's head. "Darling, I don't want you to fall out of that thing and land on this."

Tram laughed and grabbed her hand. "I promise I'll fall in a snowbank. How's that?"

"Kelly and I will be going to Anchorage in a few days," Jonathan said in the lull that followed. "While we're there, I'll have the glider kit sent out. We should see about bringing Bonnie back, too. Her leg is in a cast, but she'll be able to get around. What do you think, sweetheart? Can they manage without us for a few days?"

"I guess they'll have to," Kelly said drily. He'd done it again, she thought bitterly. He'd won over Tram and Mike with the glider and then mentioned the trip to Anchorage in a way that made it impossible for her to refuse.

They walked silently down the snow-packed path to their cabin and Kelly went to take a shower as soon as she hung up her coat. She had to admit it was nice to have hot water any time she wanted it. She stood beneath the warm stream and let the tension wash out of her. Later in bed she listened to the hiss of the water as Jonathan took his own shower. How could he possibly be content to stay in this primitive place? Why was he doing it?

She was still wondering about it when Jonathan got into bed and pulled her against his naked chest.

"Did the shower warm you up?" he asked, nuzzling her face with his lips. "Come on now. Admit it's nice to take a hot shower after coming in out of the cold."

"I never said it wasn't nice. I said we couldn't afford to run the electric tank all day. When you don't have much money, you have to be careful how you spend it."

"You don't have to be careful, darling. How can I make you understand that?"

"You can't." Her voice came out in a shaken whisper because his lips were tormenting the hollow at the base of her throat. The old familiar excitement was beginning to throb through her blood. Holding her breath so that she couldn't smell the scents of his hair and skin, she willed herself to lie perfectly still and not respond.

"You didn't have much to say about the trip to Anchorage." His lips had moved on to tantalize the tender swell of her exposed breast.

"You didn't give me any choice."

"Don't you want to see a doctor about birth control?" His thumb stroked her nipple, sending a shiver of fierce pleasure through her body.

"Yes!" she said fiercely. "But I wouldn't need to see a doctor if you . . ."

He cut off her words with his lips. "Hush! I can't

do that. Don't ask me to do the impossible." He made a hoarse sound and rolled on top of her, pushing her slender body into the softness of the bed.

Kelly couldn't hold back a groan of satisfaction that seemed to come from the pit of her stomach. Her heart was racing, her blood thundering in her ears. Her body was so taut she felt she would explode with the agony of wanting him.

Hungrily his mouth explored her parted lips, making them quiver in eager response until her own mouth opened to the sweet taste of his kisses. She touched his bare chest, his back, her hands possessive, stroking the tense muscles, hearing the blood pound in her ears, deafening her. Their kisses became harder as their naked bodies strained against each other. Kelly was terrified of the fire burning deep inside her. For a fleeting moment she considered pushing him away from her. But his body had hardened in intolerable desire, forcing her to feel the urgency of his need against her lower limbs. His hands moved down to cup her buttocks and she lost the power to resist him.

"Darling," he whispered, his voice shaking. "Kelly, Kelly, darling." His face was buried in her throat. "I've got to have . . . You'll hate me if I get you pregnant, but I've got to . . ." His mouth sought hers.

She broke off the kiss to take a shuddering

breath. "I won't hate you, Jack." She enfolded him tenderly in her arms, luxuriating in the feel of his hard shoulders against her palms.

The heat of their passion overwhelmed her. As it spread through her limbs, all the pressures that had built up within her were released. For timeless moments the love she had felt two years before broke through the barriers she had erected and surged free in a burst of uncontrollable elation. Then he was sighing and sagging against her and the tears she had held in check for so long squeezed between her tightly closed lids, wetting his chest. He rolled onto his back, taking her with him, not saying a word, just stroking her hair, her cheeks and her throat until, soothed and comforted, she drifted off to sleep.

She woke in the night to find herself alone. Deprived of that warm male body she had become accustomed to having beside her, she felt bereft. The light was on in the other room so she left her warm bed and paused in the doorway. Jonathan was standing beside the fireplace, where a fresh log lay on the grate. He stood there, a solitary, lonely figure in pajama bottoms, his feet bare, his arm resting on the mantel. As she watched, he raked a hand through his hair, tousling it, then rubbed it wearily across his forehead. He reached over and turned off the lamp, then stood staring down into the flames, the red glow flickering on his bare chest.

"Jonathan . . ."

He turned and stared at her for a long time, his eyes roaming over her face as though trying to read her thoughts. Then, as if suddenly coming to life, he moved the screen back in front of the blaze and came toward her.

"It's cold, honey. Get back in bed." In the firelight his eyes flickered over the white gleam of her body. "I got up to put on another log and discovered I had left the damper open. You're shivering."

He led her back to the bedroom, lifted the blankets, and she slid into bed. She could see her breath, it was so cold. He got in beside her and she went willingly into his arms.

"What were you thinking about standing there beside the fire?" she whispered against his skin. "Were you thinking how nice it would be in a centrally heated apartment with a cook in the kitchen to fix your breakfast and bring it to you on a tray?"

"No. Central heat and breakfast were the farthest things from my mind. But speaking of breakfast, I'd like some blueberry pancakes."

"Tough. I'm the cook and I want French toast."

"Blueberry pancakes." He poked her in the ribs and she wiggled and hid her face against his neck.

"I'd argue, but I'm too comfy. How about you?"

Jonathan smiled and held her very close. "Me, too," he whispered into her hair.

CHAPTER ELEVEN

IT SEEMED STRANGE to be sitting in the plane beside Jonathan. Kelly stole a look at him. His dark hair had grown long in the weeks he had been at the resort. Then the dark eyes that could sparkle with bitterness or amusement returned her look and he smiled, his staid features boyishly handsome. He confused her, excited her, angered her. They had little in common, except for a powerful physical bond, and here they were in his plane on their way to Anchorage just like a normal married couple.

"The trip shouldn't take over an hour," Jonathan was saying. His eyes flicked over her face, framed by the fur collar of her coat. Wisps of hair lay around her face and her eyes were large and faintly apprehensive.

Kelly looked down at the white and green landscape of forest and plains. This was rugged country, beautiful country, her country.

"Look! There's a herd of caribou." Her eyes, bright with excitement one moment turned sad the next. "They didn't even run. They've become so used to planes and helicopters they'll just stand and be slaughtered by so-called sportsmen who hunt by plane." Her voice was bitter.

"Isn't there a law against that kind of hunting?"

"Yes, but how can they enforce it in this vast

country?" She looked out the window at the patches of pine dotting the white landscape. Alaska, as she had known it, was fast disappearing, becoming a "get-rich, oil-boom" state. Soon the image of Alaska—huskies trotting across the icy tundra, Eskimos bundled up in fur parkas, trail-weary trappers, and frosty-bearded old sourdoughs—would be just a memory.

"Why does it have to be this way?" She brought her concerned eyes back to Jonathan. "Why does everything have to change? There's no sameness to anything anymore. The country changes, relationships change, people don't bother to get married unless they're having a child, don't work if they can get a handout from the government. They scar the earth, destroy the wildlife, disrupt nature's cycle, contaminate . . ."

"Hush, sweetheart. There isn't a thing we can do about most of those things. At least we're not guilty of one of them. We got married."

"Yes. We got married," she echoed, but there was no joy in her words and she turned back to the window so he wouldn't see the pain in her eyes.

The plane landed and was towed to a private hangar. A blond man with a blond mustache waited at the bottom of the steps. He and the other men working around the plane remained silent as they observed Kelly coming down the steps, Jonathan behind her, his hand tucked beneath her elbow.

"Hello, Mark. How are you standing this cold weather?"

"Not bad, sir. I don't find all that much difference between the weather here and in Boston."

"This is my wife, Mark. Sweetheart, this is Mark Lemon." Was that pride in his voice? she wondered. Surely not!

"Happy to meet you, Mrs. Templeton."

"Kelly. Call me Kelly." If the man noticed that her voice held more command than request, he didn't allow it to show.

The pilot handed out Kelly's small bag which Jonathan took from her. Mark picked up Jonathan's larger, heavier suitcase and led the way to a car parked just outside the hangar. It wasn't as big a car, or as expensive a model as the ones Jonathan used in Boston, but it was new and roomy. Somehow Kelly couldn't picture Jonathan in a small compact car. Mark stowed the luggage in the trunk.

"Can you catch a ride into town with Tom if we go on alone?" Jonathan asked.

"I'm sure I can." Mark turned to call to the pilot. "Going into town, Tom?"

"Sure thing."

Mark handed the car keys to Jonathan and opened the door for Kelly.

"There's a couple of urgent matters I'd like to discuss, sir," he said when Kelly was seated.

"They'll have to wait, Mark. I'll call the office

tomorrow. Did you have any trouble making the arrangements I requested?" he asked sharply.

"No, sir. None at all, but . . ."

"Anything else can wait." Jonathan opened the door and folded his long length into the car. He glanced at Kelly briefly before starting the motor and following the arrows out of the parking ramp, then easing the car into the stream of traffic.

"Anything you especially want to do?" he asked, breaking the silence between them.

"There's a few friends I'd like to phone. You never did tell me how long we'll be here." She tried not to sound accusing, but it came out that way.

"I'd like to stay four days. It's the middle of the week and we're not needed at the resort."

"Four days! I can't possibly stay four days. I thought this was an overnight trip. I only brought one other outfit besides the one I'm wearing."

"Is that all that's bothering you? Don't they have clothing stores in Anchorage?" His hand left the wheel and caressed her knee. "We can get you outfitted without any bother at all."

"I don't want to be outfitted like an orphan dragged in out of the boonies! I prefer my own clothes, thank you!" She faced him angrily. "I thought I was coming here to see a gynecologist and to be fitted with a contraceptive shield. That's the *only* reason I'm here."

"Why are you so angry? What's so unusual

about a man wanting to buy clothes for his wife?" He pushed down on the gas pedal and the car shot forward.

"We're not a normal married couple, and you know it. You have your life and I have mine."

"That's not true. We've been living together. Doesn't that count for something?"

"We've been sleeping together. There's a difference."

He muttered a curse and turned to her, his eyes glittering with suppressed anger. A van cut in front of them and he jammed on the brake, swearing mightily.

"Good grief, Kelly! Marriage is a two way street and if I'm willing to give a little, you should do the same."

"If you'll remember, Jonathan, I never asked you to 'give a little.' It was your idea to resume our . . . our married status. I was perfectly content with my life and ready to sign the divorce papers. I'll admit it was petty of me to not let you know where I was. But I had eight miserable months with you and I was just human enough to want someone to suffer for it."

He was silent for a long moment. "It was that bad?"

"Yes, Jonathan, it was." She felt no joy in telling him.

He looked at her briefly again. "I'm sorry I made you so unhappy," he said softly.

She felt drained of all emotion. "It wasn't all

154

your fault. I shouldn't have married you until I knew what would be expected of me."

They arrived at a parking ramp when Jonathan rolled down the window and said, "Jonathan Templeton." Immediately the door opened into the underground parking area and they were escorted to a space near the elevator. Two uniformed attendents hastened to help them out while another spoke on the telephone.

"Mr. Templeton is here," he announced importantly.

Suddenly the whole situation struck Kelly as funny and she burst out laughing. Jonathan looked down at her with surprise and confusion.

"What's so funny?" His tone wiped the grin from her face.

"You wouldn't understand, Jonathan."

"Try me," he insisted.

She ignored him and followed the attendent into the elevator. Jonathan entered too and handed the man a bill.

"I'll take them from here."

As the elevator rose, long forgotten memories came rushing back to Kelly. The door opened, Jonathan picked up both bags, and, without looking at her, led the way down a short hallway. He set the bags down, and opened the door, and before Kelly could catch her breath, he had picked her up and carried her into the room. He set her on her feet and stood looking down at her.

"Hello," he said softly.

She looked at him with stricken eyes before turning away to hide her tears. The room was just like it had been before. Two dozen roses stood on a table beside the bed. A bottle of champagne rested in a bucket of ice. A filmy white nightdress was draped over the chair. Her eyes fastened onto the nightdress and she said the first thing that came to mind.

"I'm not a virgin this time."

Jonathan pulled her to him. "And I'm responsible for that, too." He kissed her gently, tenderly, and let her go when she moved to leave his arms. "You have an appointment with the doctor in . . ." he looked at his watch ". . . forty-five minutes. Would you like to shower? You can use all the hot water you want."

Watching various expressions flit across his face, Kelly thought of his arrogance, and the high-handed methods he had used to get what he wanted. But his persistence disarmed her.

"I wish I knew what was going on inside that head of yours," he murmured, almost as if to himself.

"I was thinking of the electric bill if they heat all the water used here with electricity."

"Liar!" The way he said the word made it more a caress than a censure. He took her coat from her and gave her a gentle push. "Time is fleeting, woman. Take your shower, or I'll be in there with you and we'll miss the appointment altogether."

Standing under the warm water, Kelly thought of the last time she had stood here—with Jack. They had soaped each other, frolicked and played like two kids, and finally come together as one under the sensuous spray. On that day she had never imagined life would be anything but beautiful. She stepped out of the shower, toweled herself dry, and slipped into clean underwear, willing herself not to think of anything but the present.

They went down in the elevator together and walked across the lobby past elegantly dressed matrons, tourists, and young executives hurrying by with expensive briefcases tucked under their arms. The weather was comparatively warm and Kelly walked beside Jonathan, her coat open and her head bare.

"Do you want to walk or take a taxi? It's only a couple of blocks."

"I'd rather walk. And I can go alone. You needn't come with me."

"I don't have anything else to do." He took her elbow and they stepped onto the sidewalk. Kelly lifted her face to the slight breeze blowing through her hair. She was glad she had come. She liked the city. This was where she'd live if she had to leave the resort. Her eyes took in the sights and her nose the smells, all familiar to her. They walked past the office building where she and Jack had first collided. If he noticed or remembered, he didn't give any indication of it. Minutes later Kelly left Jonathan sitting in the waiting room of the Medical Building and was ushered into the doctor's office.

When she came out again, Jonathan was talking to a small boy with a cast on his arm. They were deep in conversation and Kelly hesitated before interrupting.

"It was that dumb old Chad that did it. He dumped me off his bike. Shouldn't have been riding on the handlebars, my mom said." The small boy was standing between Jonathan's knees looking earnestly into his face.

"Your mom is right. It was a dumb thing to do. How long do you have to stay trussed up like that?"

"The doc said I'd get it off before Christmas."

"Good. Just in time to help Santa Claus deliver presents."

"There ain't no Santa Claus. That's what Chad said." The boy's bright eyes were fastened on Jonathan's face.

"I'm beginning to believe you're right about Chad being dumb. You believe in the tooth fairy and goblins on Halloween, don't you?"

"Yeah. I got a quarter under my pillow when I lost this tooth." He opened his mouth wide. "Mom said the tooth fairy left it."

"Well, what do you know. I wasn't sure there was a tooth fairy."

"Yeah, there is. I put the quarter in my bank. I wanted to buy bubble gum, but mom said no."

Jonathan got up and put his hand on the boy's head. "We've settled that then, haven't we, scout?"

"Settled what? And my name is Amos."

"I thought we'd decided Chad was dumb, your mom right, and that there really is a Santa Claus."

The boy gave a toothless grin. "Yeah."

Jonathan lifted Kelly's coat from the hook, the boy following after him.

"You got any kids, mister?"

"No, but I've got a wife."

"Oh." The boy looked at Kelly and dismissed her. "I was gonna tell ya that if ya had kids to tell 'em not to ride on the handlebars."

"Well, if I had any, I'd be sure to tell them. Bye, scout. Take care of yourself."

"My name's Amos," the boy called as they went out the door.

"Some conversation," Kelly commented as they walked the narrow hallway.

"He was a dandy. All boy." His face was pensive for a moment, then he smiled down at her. "Everything okay with you? Did you get what you came for?" She nodded and he put an arm across her shoulders and squeezed. "I hope it's a good strong one. It's going to get a lot of use."

Kelly blushed to the roots of her hair and tried to look cross and failed. "You've got a one track mind."

"Two tracks. I'm hungry. How about pizza?"

"Sure."

They paused for the traffic light to change, then strode across the wide street.

"What about tonight?"

"What about it?"

"Where do you want to eat? What do you think I meant?"

"I didn't know what track you were on. I don't care where we eat as long as it isn't fancy."

"How about the room? We can have something sent up. Maybe there's a sexy movie on closed-circuit television." She laughed up at him, he grinned down at her, and they ran into a man carrying a large bundle. Jonathan apologized and they continued down the street.

The movie was a comedy. In spite of herself, Kelly found herself enjoying it. They had eaten a delicious meal, shared a bottle of wine, and thumbed through the current newspapers. Now curled up against the big fluffy pillows, Kelly watched television while Jonathan lounged on the end of the bed. Instead of the filmy white nightdress, she wore a nightshirt that came down to her knees. Always in her memory were the other nights she had spent in this room. Here she had reached boundless heights of ecstasy and lived her happiest moments.

She was so absorbed in her own thoughts that the movie ended and she continued to stare at the long list of credits. She was only half-aware of Jonathan reaching for the remote control button and stretching out a hand to stroke one finger down her cheek with a featherlight touch. Her thoughts shifted as he moved up close to her, disturbingly, tantalizingly handsome in his pajama bottoms, his chest bare, his freshly washed hair fluffy from the hair dryer.

"I don't think you realize how sweet an invitation you are, sitting there in your nightshirt . . . your eyes all dreamy . . . your mouth soft . . ."

She didn't move and he drew her against him, bending his head and hesitating for an unbearable moment before touching her lips. All the emotional bruising of the time spent in Boston and the months since flowed and melted away under the balm of his lips. Her mouth clung in a moment of incredible sweetness.

Very softly she said, "Jack."

He lifted his head and was perfectly still, letting his eyes, soft with love, drink in her face. Then, with a deep sigh, he took her in his arms and held her close, her head buried in his shoulder, while he gently stroked her hair. He didn't say a word, but turned her face to his and kissed her mouth, fiercely, passionately. Kelly closed her eyes and moved sensuously closer to him.

His lips left hers and he looked directly into her eyes, a faint smile softening his mouth.

"This is the woman I married," he murmured. "Soft, sweet, but spunky, willful . . ."

In a sort of fascination she watched his hands slide over her body and lift the nightshirt up and over her head. He moved her down until she lay across the bed. The soft light of the lamp shone on his hair as he bent his head. She felt the feathery touch of it against her skin, then the warm caress of his lips in the curve of her neck.

Sudden tears ached behind her eyes. She moved her hand to the back of his head and gently stroked his hair.

"It isn't the same, is it?" she whispered into the cheek pressed to her lips.

"No, darling," he said between kisses. "It's better. Much better." This was not the cold-eyed Boston businessman speaking. This was Jack, her lover: tender and affectionate, his eyes warm with love.

From then on nothing mattered except satisfying their desperate need for each other. They swirled in a mindless vortex of pleasure created by caressing fingertips, biting teeth, and closely entwined limbs. It was long and rapturous, that worshipping of bodies, and when they finally came together, it was forceful, but ecstatic and only momentarily satisfying. Time and again he drew her to him, seemingly tireless, murmuring softly of the hunger that gnawed at him and the thirst for the mouth she offered so willingly.

They made love deep into the night, until sheer exhaustion sent Jonathan into a deep sleep and Kelly into that void between sleep and awareness. As she lay molded to his body, her head resting on his chest, she finally accepted that Jonathan was Jack and she loved him. She wept silently.

CHAPTER TWELVE

"GOOD MORNING, SLEEPING BEAUTY." Jonathan's voice spoke softly in her ear. She opened one eye. Light filled the room, gilding the red roses on the bedside table. She opened the other eye and surveyed the pale yellow walls, rich mahogany furniture . . . and a gorgeous male body bending over hers. She ran her fingertips lightly over his chest, as if to make sure he was real. He was. She smiled, then yawned and stretched.

"I've been waiting half an hour. I thought you'd never wake up!" He sounded more like a small boy than a lover, and she laughed.

"I was tired." She smiled again and let her fingers move across his chest to a nipple. It had been a long, delicious night.

"Complaining?"

"Are you kidding me?"

He looked tenderly into her eyes, and there was something in his face she hadn't seen for a long while—a kind of unfettered love she had thought she would never see again.

"I love you, Kelly . . . love you . . ." His words melted on her lips and when she tried to speak, her words kept fading, swept away by his kisses.

"Jonathan . . ."

"Don't say anything." His lips covered hers before she could speak. "Are you sleepy, darling?" His voice was a whisper when they finally broke the kiss. She was curled up in his arms, one leg braided between his.

"Mm-hmm . . . Jonathan?"

"Yes, love?"

"What are we going to do?"

"We're going to take one day at a time, sweetheart." His voice was soft and his warm breath tickled her ear.

"But, Jonathan . . ."

"Shhh . . ."

"Jonathan . . ." This time she forgot what she was going to say as his body slid slowly over hers and she was swept away, adrift on a cloud of sensation as his whole being seemed to enter hers.

Two more hours passed as they made love, dozed, and made love again. Then they were standing beneath the stinging spray of the shower, laughing about the luxurious use of hot water, soaping each other, teasing. She lifted her face for his kiss and the stream of water hit her full in the face.

"I'll drown," she gasped.

He grasped her soap slick body and pulled it tight against him. "What a way to go!"

"You're obscene!" she giggled and leaned her forehead against his chest.

Kelly's happy glow lasted all through the breakfast brought to their room by a white-coated busboy. She ate as if she were starved, finishing off tiny sausages, fluffy eggs, and a Danish roll dripping with melted butter. They smiled into each other's eyes often and, when possible, Jonathan reached out to touch her thigh, her arm, or flutter fingertips across her cheek.

"Still want to go back to the resort today?" he asked. They were drinking coffee, the breakfast dishes having been removed.

"I can't wear these clothes for four days."

"You won't have to. Your clothes are here. I had them shipped out from Boston." He watched her anxiously.

"Why did you do that?" There was a shadow of concern in her eyes.

"I wanted you to have them. I lived in an apartment here in Anchorage for a month before coming out to the resort. I can't turn loose everything all at once, no matter how much I want to. The apartment serves as a headquarters along with the office I established here. I brought all your things there. I wanted you to have them . . . no matter what."

The tender regard in his eyes made her hand

tremble as she reached out to him. He took her hand silently. What could she say?

"What are you thinking?" His voice was strained.

"Okay."

"Okay, what?"

"Okay, I'll put on my glad-rags and we'll do up the town." She smiled wickedly at him and caressed him with her eyes. He looked as happy as a small boy and she wanted to throw her arms around him.

"Shall we go to the apartment? You can cook my breakfast tomorrow morning. Blueberry pancakes."

"Can I take the roses?"

"The hotel will send them over with the rest of our things. First I've got to go to the office and take care of a few urgent matters. At least Mark thinks they're urgent." He handed her a key from his pocket. "Take a cab and I'll meet you there in a couple of hours." He scribbled an address on a card. "Tell the doorman who you are and he'll take care of you."

After pausing beside the desk to leave instructions about the bill and their luggage, they left the hotel together. Jonathan put Kelly in a waiting taxi, handed the driver some money, and gave the address of the apartment building. He stood on the sidewalk and watched the cab drive away.

Kelly was in love again and gloriously happy. She smiled to herself, her blue eyes dancing, her face reflecting the warm glow of feeling loved. How had she allowed Jack and Jonathan to become two separate people in her mind? A little tremor trilled down her spine. Thank God he had forced her to make this trip. It would be hard to wait until she could be with him again.

A blast of horns brought her from her reverie. The taxi dodged into a lane of traffic, crossed a busy intersection, made its way down a tree-lined street of apartment buildings, and pulled into a circular drive. The building was ultra-modern and ultra-expensive, Kelly thought without cynicism. She had become a reverse snob, she admitted reluctantly. It wasn't Jonathan's fault he was born with a silver spoon in his mouth, anymore than it was hers that she wasn't.

Kelly crossed to the large, glass door that opened automatically as she approached. The inside of the building fairly screamed the word "exclusive" and the man who came to meet her looked like the maître d' at some posh French restaurant.

"May I be of help?" His tone clearly implied that she had wandered into the wrong building. Kelly bristled.

"I'm Mrs. Jonathan Templeton. Will you direct me to our apartment? My husband will be along in a couple of hours."

"I'm afraid I'll need identification, madam." He stood in front of her as if guarding the Mint.

"My key." She showed it to him and dug into her purse. "My driver's license." Pure deviltry made her add, "Will you need to frisk me?"

His face turned a dull red and she was instantly sorry for her flip words.

"I'm sorry, Mrs. Templeton. Rules . . ."

"No. *I'm* sorry. I understand the need for such rules." She smiled so sweetly that the stern face almost relaxed.

He led the way down the thickly carpeted hallway, paused beside a table holding a beautiful potted plant and pushed a button. Paneled doors opened silently and Kelly stepped into the elevator.

"Insert your key in number five on the panel, ma'am. The elevator will take you to the fifth floor."

"And?"

"Yours is the only apartment on that floor."

"Oh . . . Thank you, very much."

The door closed. Kelly inserted her key and the cage moved. In mere seconds it slid to a gentle stop and the door opened. She faced another door with the name plate "Jonathan Templeton." She stood for a moment, her eyes riveted. Would she ever get used to what money could do?

The key turned silently in the lock and the door swung open to reveal a room right out of a decorating magazine. Nothing was out of place. The delicate green silk on the sofa was smoothed to perfection and the soft matching pillows were tilted at just the right angle. Louis XV chairs, tables on delicately carved legs, silk-shaded lamps all stood on a Persian carpet of muted greens, faded rose, and soft blue. The music coming from the intercom went so perfectly with the room that she scarcely noticed it.

Kelly closed the door and went to stand in the center of the room. It seemed a sacrilege to walk on the carpet. Jonathan must employ a live-in housekeeper. Everything was perfect. The plants, which were set in just the right places, would need constant care. She moved through a formal dining room toward swinging doors, then veered around the table toward an arched opening from which came the soft murmur of voices.

Her feet refused to carry her past the doorway. It was as if they were suddenly glued to the floor. Momentarily she could feel nothing and she stood as if the breath had been knocked out of her. Katherine and Nancy were seated at a small table, a coffee service between them.

"Oh!" Katherine looked up, startled. "Oh!" she said again and Nancy swung around to stare too. Katherine gained her composure first. "What do you want? What do you mean coming in here like that? You frightened me!" At first her voice was breathless, then accusing.

A wave of sickness rose into Kelly's throat. She fought it down, knowing Jonathan had sent her here, alone, to face his hostile sister.

"What do you want? Can't you say anything?" Nancy's thin face showed bitter resentment.

"Hush, Nancy. I'll handle this." The rebuke was gentle, but failed to erase the belligerence from her stepdaughter's face. "Jonathan isn't here." Katherine stood up, moved to the back of her chair, and gripped it with ringed fingers. "He's out of town. He sent word yesterday that he won't be back for a week."

"How long have you been here?" Pride and anger were replacing sickness and betrayal.

"What do you mean, how long have we been here? We came as soon as Jonathan found a suitable apartment for us. In his position he needs social contacts, and Nancy and I are his family, in case you've forgotten." Her thin mouth quivered.

"I can hardly forget that gruesome fact," Kelly said drily, pleased that she could speak at all.

"Don't be vulgar." Kelly felt a small triumph at having upset Katherine's composure even a little but it vanished when her sister-in-law spoke again. "Are you still trying to get a large settlement out of Jonathan?"

"And . . . if I am?"

"He's prepared to be generous, although he has ways of reducing it. Jonathan does have his pride. It's hard for him to admit he made a mistake by marrying you." Katherine's contemptuous eyes never left Kelly's face.

The silence lengthened. Kelly refused to let Katherine see how coldly angry she was. She noted with satisfaction that Katherine's cheeks were flushed. She was nervous and frightened but Kelly intended to stay.

"Have you seen Jonathan?" Nancy faced Kelly like a spitting cat.

"Of course," Kelly replied flippantly, though her heart was breaking. "How do you think I got the key?" She dangled it from her fingers.

"Did you come to get your things? He said he brought them here. He didn't want you showing up in Boston to get them. You had created enough embarrassment for him."

"He needn't have worried."

"I'm glad you've finally realized you have no place in Jonathan's life. He and Nancy are going to be married as soon as the divorce is final. Probably before Christmas." Katherine looked directly into Kelly's eyes and spoke with deliberation. "We are all anxious to put this distasteful episode behind us. And if it means a large settlement, so be it."

"I understand completely."

"I thought you would." Katherine moved past her down a long hall to a door at the far end. As she opened the door, Kelly walked past her and shut and locked it in the woman's face. She leaned against it, closed her eyes, and breathed deeply. Anger put her feet in motion and she went to the large wardrobe at the end of the room and swung open the double doors. The clothes she had left in Boston were hanging on neat racks—blouses, slacks, daydresses, and evening clothes all grouped together with rows of shoes underneath.

Kelly grabbed an armload of dresses and carried them to the bed, then searched through the vanity for scissors. She began cutting the expensive garments in two pieces, separating them at the waist and dropping them to the floor. When the bed was empty, she returned to the closet for more clothes and kept cutting until her thumb throbbed. All at once she wanted to cry. She let the scissors fall to the floor and picked up her purse, ashamed of her childish act.

She left the room, locking the door behind her. Nancy and Katherine were standing in the living room. Katherine's face was pale and strained; Nancy's was still belligerent. Outwardly composed, Kelly managed a sardonic smile and dropped the apartment key in a glass dish on the coffee table, then walked directly to the door, forcing the older woman to step out of her way.

"Tell Jonathan he can keep the clothes for Nancy if he'll increase my settlement another twenty thousand." She closed the door softly behind her, and walked down the five flights of emergency stairs to the main lobby. She smiled brightly at the man at the desk and went out onto the street. She knew exactly what she was going to do. She was going home!

A taxi took her to the railway station. Before boarding the train, she placed a call to the station manager in Hurricane and asked him to contact Mike by radio and have him meet her. Thirty minutes later, she was on her way.

Retreating farther and farther into her thoughts, Kelly hardly noticed the landscape passing outside her window. Her heart ached for her lost love, but her pride was wounded as well. Jonathan had deliberately set about to win her back. Once he'd succeeded, he'd sent her to the apartment to collect his revenge. She hoped the taste was bitter in his mouth. It wasn't money he wanted. When she'd left him, his pride, too, had suffered a terrific blow that wouldn't allow him to rest until he had damaged hers.

Kelly's eyes were hot and dry, but she refused to close them for fear the tears would come. She refused to shed useless tears.

The train rolled on, passing station after station, the click of the wheels singing a familiar tune. But Kelly's thoughts were far away. Now she would have to tell Mike and Marty that Jonathan owned the resort. Eventually his agents would arrive to dispossess them. She calculated mentally. They should have until December to vacate the property. If Jonathan intended to marry Nancy by

Christmas, he must have already started divorce proceedings.

The miles flew by and finally the train pulled into the station at Talkeetna. It was dark when Kelly stepped off, dark at only four o'clock in the afternoon. She pulled the fur collar of her jacket up around her face and walked toward Mike, who was waiting at the end of the platform. Her eyes were glued to his face as she approached. She walked into his arms and hid her face against his shoulder.

"Oh, Mike. I've been such a fool!"

"Yeah."

At last she pulled away from him and he took her hand. He led her to the waiting utility truck, whose running motor sent out a cloud of white fog. Kelly slipped into the passenger seat and Mike revved up the engine. Kelly didn't speak until they were on the highway.

"I have something to tell you, Mike. It isn't going to be easy for me to say, or for you to hear, but it's got to be said. When I married Jonathan, I signed papers allowing him to handle the probate of Daddy's will, and then I completely forgot about it until he reminded me of it when he first came to the resort. He also told me he'd paid six years of back taxes. Now the property is legally his." She waited for the explosion that was sure to follow.

Mike was silent for a long while. "That . . . bastard!" He hissed the words from between clenched teeth.

"I'm sorry, Mike. I'm so sorry. My stupidity has cheated you and Marty out of your share. I was so gullible!"

"Join the crowd," Mike said wearily. "I was even beginning to like the bastard."

"What are we going to do? How are we going to tell Marty?" She felt, rather than heard, the soft groan that came from her throat.

Mike glanced at her, then took her hand. "She's a big girl. She'll take her lumps along with the rest of us."

"But she and Tram gave up their jobs in Fairbanks. Oh, why didn't I stay in Portland?"

"Maybe we can raise the money to buy him out." Mike was grasping at straws and they both knew it.

"He'd never sell to us. He's out for revenge and he's got us in the palm of his hot little hand." Her words were bitter.

"What happened?"

She knew what he meant, but couldn't bring herself to tell him. "Nothing much. He led me down the primrose path, then pushed me into the icy slough."

"I knew something had happened when you called."

After that they were silent. Mike concentrated on the highway that was becoming slick with a freezing mist. Kelly buried her hands deep in the pockets of her coat and stared straight ahead. She felt better now that she had told Mike about the property, and she promised herself that somehow, someday, she would make it up to him and Marty.

"Drop me off at Marty's, Mike," she said when they turned into the driveway. "I've got to tell her and I'd better do it now."

Mike parked beside Marty's cabin. The air was crisp and the tangy, familiar scent of woodsmoke invaded Kelly's nostrils. This was home. She wished she'd never left it.

Marty opened the door before they reached it. "What in the world happened?"

Kelly stomped the snow from her street shoes and took off her coat before she answered. "Plenty!"

"I figured that. You look as if you've been through a wringer. Why in the world did you come back alone. Jonathan . . ."

"I never want to set eyes on him again!" Once again, tears burned in her eyes.

"Well I'm afraid you're going to see him, because he's here."

Kelly's head jerked around. "Here? I don't believe it!"

"Believe it. He flew in right after Mike left to pick you up. And he's raving mad!"

"That's too damn bad. So am I!" Kelly walked over to the warm, cheery fire and turned her back to it. Mike took off his coat and boots. Tram stood beside his chair and watched her with gentle eyes.

"Tell us what happened, for heaven's sake," Marty demanded. "I've been so worried since Jonathan came storming in here demanding to know if we'd heard from you." Her face was creased with concern.

"Jonathan and I have irreconcilable differences. I don't want to discuss them. But I've got something else to tell you." She told them that Jonathan now controlled the resort. "Marty, Tram, I'm so sorry. I don't know what else to say. I wanted you to know the worst right away so you could make plans."

Marty looked as if she would burst into tears. "You can't mean he'll boot us out of here? But . . . this is home!" She turned angrily to Mike. "Why didn't you take care of those taxes? We could have raked up the money somehow."

"I didn't know they were overdue. I thought they'd been taken out of the estate."

"Don't blame Mike. Blame me." Kelly said wearily. "There's one small bit of good news. Jonathan may own the property, but he doesn't own the business or the furnishings. Maybe he'll give you enough for them so you can get a new start somewhere else."

"It isn't that," Marty wailed. "I don't think I could bear it if I didn't know that home was here and I could come back to it when I wanted to."

The anguish in her tone tore at Kelly's heart and she wished for words to comfort her. But before she could think of any, the door opened and Jonathan stepped into the room.

All the anger and humiliation she had felt in the apartment came boiling up. Her angry eyes locked with his across the room. He stood inside the door in his sheepskin coat, his bare head dusted with a sprinkling of snow. He acted as if there was no one else in the room. The silence lengthened and became heavy with tension.

"Am I being excluded from the conference?" He spoke to everyone, but his eyes remained on Kelly.

"Yes!" Kelly cried. "You most certainly are excluded!" She hadn't intended to speak so bitterly. She wanted to be calm, uncaring. "I've told them you own the resort."

"I see," he said quietly.

"No, you don't *see* anything. You're too stiff-necked to see down to our level, but if you could, you would realize that we'll survive together. We have each other. Who do you have, Jonathan? Katherine and Nancy?"

"I'd rather discuss our misunderstanding in private." He removed her coat from the hook and came toward her. She met him in the middle of the room and snatched it from his hand.

"We've said it! The next time I speak to you will be before the divorce judge. Or do you have the clout to divorce me without a hearing?" Her anger was intensified by the stricken look that crossed his face. What an actor he was! He started to follow her to the door but she turned on him like a spitting cat. "Stay away from me! I'm going home . . . to my house! If he tries to follow me, Mike, break his leg!" At the door, she turned with a parting remark. "I want you out of here tomorrow. All debtors are allowed thirty days to vacate and we're taking every day of that time." Her lungs felt as if they were about to explode, but she managed one more breath. "You come near my cabin and I'll . . . I'll fill you with buckshot!"

Kelly slammed the door and ran across the snow-packed yard to her own front door. The lamp was lit and a new log lay on the hot coals in the fireplace. Thank goodness her father had made a bar to go across the door. She went to the closet to get it, then placed a chair beneath the knob on the rear door. Only then did she take off her coat and slip out of her wet shoes.

CHAPTER THIRTEEN

THE NEXT FEW days were the longest and most unhappy Kelly had ever experienced.

The morning after she had locked herself in the cabin, she heard Jonathan's voice on the C.B. radio calling Hurricane. He requested they send for his plane. Then he called her.

179

"Kelly, are you on the channel?"

She turned off the set.

It was almost noon when she heard the plane land in the clearing. Still in her nightgown and robe, she went to the window. Tram took Jonathan to the clearing in the pickup and returned. Kelly stood by the window, tears streaming down her face. A part of her life was over. She cried for lost dreams, for the agony of disillusionment. She had to face the fact that her long-cherished idea of love was simply a myth, that the kind of love she wanted didn't exist except in the imagination of poets and novelists.

During the long day when she sat beside the fire or lay on the couch hoping for the sleep that eluded her, memories of the scene with Katherine and Nancy stayed doggedly in her brain. She relived each word they'd said over and over again and each time she asked herself how she had ever allowed herself to get involved in such a humiliating situation. When she finally dozed, a pounding on the door awakened her.

"Kelly . . . Kelly . . . open the door," came Marty's voice.

Kelly got up off the couch. The room was cold and she shivered as she lifted the bar and opened the door.

"Good heavens! You look like you died . . . days ago."

"I did."

Marty handed her a pan wrapped in a heavy towel and took off her coat and boots. "It's cold in here."

"I know. I was sleeping."

Marty took the pan into the kitchen. "You didn't even start the cookstove," she wailed.

Kelly almost smiled. Marty tended to over-dramatize. She built up the fire while Marty tackled the cookstove, muttering and complaining all the while.

"And I thought you'd welcome me and your supper with open arms. What do I find but you lying on your fanny and the fires almost out and . . ."

"Oh, Marty! Stop that and say what you came to say."

"Okay. Why didn't you come up to the lodge and eat with the rest of us? Your leg isn't broken!"

"I didn't want to!"

"Oh!" Marty seemed to relent. "In that case," she said with her impish grin, more relaxed now, "I'm glad I came."

Half an hour later, Kelly announced, "The stew was delicious." She set the empty bowl in the sink.

"Of course. It's my best recipe, and about the only thing I'm sure will turn out well. It's a good thing Tram isn't hard to please. He'll eat anything that doesn't bite him first." Marty settled down in a chair and pulled her feet up under her. "We've decided to get me pregnant." She giggled. "Tram says he'll work on the project day and night."

"You're lucky." Kelly handed Marty a cup of coffee.

"So are you."

"Oh, yeah? Sure I am!" She avoided Marty's eyes.

"I think he loves you," Marty said softly. When Kelly didn't answer, she added, "He didn't take the property from us."

Kelly turned huge, luminous blue eyes to Marty. "What do you mean?"

"After you left last night, I thought Mike was going to kill him . . . and I would have helped. It was Tram who calmed us all down. He's not a violent person. His motto is 'talk first, fight later.' Anyway, the crux of it is this . . . Jonathan paid up the taxes and settled the inheritance tax, or we would have had to sell some of the property to pay it. But the property still belongs to us. Jonathan said we could consider it a loan at low interest."

"Don't believe him. He doesn't do anything out of the goodness of his heart. He's lulled you into believing that, but he'll lower the boom on you if things don't go the way he wants them to go. I know him. He's devious. He's divorcing me so he can marry his sister's stepdaughter. Maybe he's going to give me our property as a settlement," Kelly added with a dry laugh.

"I think he loves you."

"Don't say that! You don't know what you're talking about. I've lived with him. I know him better than you do."

"Okay, okay. You don't have to jump down my throat."

"I'm sorry. I feel so washed out. I feel as if everything has stopped but me, and I'm still whirling around in confusion, fear, and despair. Stay by me, Marty. Someday it'll be over and I'll look back on this time in my life as if it had happened to someone else. I just don't want you and Mike to build up false hopes about this place. I won't believe we still have it until the deed is in our hands."

Marty studied Kelly intently. "Time will tell," she said lightly and rose to her feet. "Meanwhile, we've got guests coming this weekend. Two wildlife photographers and a couple who want to ride on a dogsled. Tram will take care of the shutterbugs and Mike said his team is ready to supply the rides. You and I will have to cook and clean. You do the cooking."

"I hate to cook."

"So do I. But you're better at it than I am."

"I think you can do better than you let on. Aunt Mary taught us both at the same time."

"I didn't pay as much attention to the lessons as you did."

"Oh, get out of here!" Kelly's voice was warm with affection. "I'll be up in the morning to give you a hand."

Marty smiled tiredly and suppressed a yawn. "I'll need it."

Kelly worked furiously the next day, trying to tire herself out so she could sleep that night. She carried out ashes, scrubbed and cleaned, washed and ironed. When she could find nothing else to do, she started up the small chainsaw and cut the small chunks of wood needed for the cookstove. Not once did she allow herself to think of Jonathan. Her arms grew so tired holding the chainsaw that she dropped it and almost sawed into her leg. She was sensible enough to know it was dangerous to work, so she hitched Charlie to her old sled and they rode around the yard.

Charlie loved it, and Kelly began to doubt Mike's judgment that Charlie would never make a good sled dog. She told him so that evening during dinner.

"I hitched Charlie to my old sled, Mike, and he took to it like he was born to it."

"He was." Mike helped himself to another serving of potatoes.

"Well?" Kelly prompted when it became apparent he wasn't going to say more.

Marty groaned. "Mike hasn't outgrown his childish habits. You have to pull every word out of him."

Mike grinned at Kelly. "Humor me."

"Get out of here! I should take a club to you."

Tram looked at Marty questioningly. She laughed. "Don't worry, darling. They won't kill each other. This has been going on since they were ten years old."

"If I told them everything I know, Tram, they'd be as smart as me." Mike waved his fork at the girls.

"Oh, stop that and tell me." Kelly knew the twins were trying to raise her spirits, and she appreciated their concern.

"No sense of humor," Mike grumbled. "Charlie's sire was the lead dog of a team that placed in the Iditarod Trail Race a few years back."

"You're kidding!" Marty cried. She turned to Tram. "You wouldn't know about this, honey. You haven't been in Alaska long enough to know about the World Championship Dogsled Races. If a dog has the stamina to even finish that thousand mile race, his value goes up, up, up." She turned puzzled eyes to her brother. "Hey! How in the world did you manage to get Charlie?"

"Charlie's got a flaw. He's not a fighter. If I let that team of mine loose, they'd make dog meat of him. He won't even fight on a one-to-one basis."

"How about stud service?" Kelly suggested.

"No good there either. He's sterile."

"I like him. He's my dog. You gave him to me," Kelly said defiantly.

"You can have him, but keep him away from my team when I have them hitched. They're hard enough to handle as it is."

The next morning Kelly played an extra long time with Charlie. He jumped, barked, chased the frisbee until his tongue was hanging out. Kelly knelt down in the snow and hugged his shaggy neck.

"You and I are alike, Charlie. We didn't fit into what was expected of us."

At noon a delivery van backed up to the door of the lodge. Kelly saw it pull away a few minutes later and dismissed it from her mind. Probably someone asking directions. An hour passed before she went up to the lodge with a bundle of laundry and noticed that tire tracks in the snow led right up to the door. She opened it to see a mountain of crates and boxes with Marty, Mike, and Tram standing in the middle of them.

"What's going on?" she gasped. Guilt was written all over Marty's face. "Marty! What's all this stuff?"

"Now don't get in a stew. Jonathan sent out a few things. It'll be added to what we owe him," she said quickly.

"A few things?" Kelly edged her way between the boxes. "Washer, dryer, dishwasher, vacuum cleaner, microwave oven, sheets, towels . . ." She stopped reading aloud, but continued making the rounds of the boxes that filled half the family room. "And an antenna. That's so you can pull in that Tulsa, Oklahoma station and hear the football games, isn't it," she said sarcastically. Her eyes followed a path of melted snow to the back rooms.

"Kelly . . ." Marty called before her husband hushed her.

Stacks of boxes lined one wall of the big dormitory room. They were uniform in size, and the name Jonathan Templeton was stamped on each one. Kelly stood numbly looking at them. He was moving in, invading her home. He wouldn't be satisfied until he'd taken everything from her. Returning to the family room to retrieve the bundle of laundry she'd dropped, she wondered vaguely if she looked like she felt—as if she'd been kicked in the throat.

"Don't look like that, Kelly! I can't bear it!" Marty cried.

Kelly waved a weak hand at the clutter of boxes. "Money talks. I can see where that leaves me."

"Don't you dare say that!" Marty broke away from Tram and rushed over to her. "We needed things to make this place pay. It's a loan, Kelly. Just a loan."

"Then what're his things doing back there?" She jerked her head toward the bedrooms.

"We couldn't very well refuse to rent the dormitory. Be reasonable, Kelly," Marty pleaded.

"Did you agree to this, Mike?"

Mike remained silent and his sister prompted him angrily.

"Tell her! Tell her the three of us talked it over with Jonathan and agreed the place needed refurbishing."

"Oh, hush, Marty! Yes, I agreed, Kelly. Business is business." Mike didn't look at her.

"I thought I was a partner in this venture, too," Kelly whispered through stiff lips. "Don't I have say about something as important as this?"

"We knew what you'd say," Mike said stubbornly.

"I hope you enjoy all this." Kelly waved her hand at the boxes again and went out the door before they could see that she was trembling. "Oh, Tram!" she heard Marty wail.

Kelly forced her trembling legs to support her down the path and was grateful for the cold air she sucked into her lungs. She prayed the leaden weight in the pit of her stomach would dissolve.

Inside the sanctuary of her own home, she threw herself down on the couch. Great, shuddering sobs tore through her. It was a relief to let the misery flow out of her. She could cry here. There was no one to see her. The tears came in an overwhelming flood, pouring down her cheeks and seeping between her fingers.

At last the tears stopped and she lay on the couch staring into the fire. She was tired. She put another chunk of wood on the grate, went to her room, and changed into her long flannel gown. She took her pillow and down-filled comforter back to the couch, and fell asleep almost instantly.

Kelly woke early the next morning. The room was so cold she could see her breath. She got out from under the warm blankets, put more wood on the fire, turned on the electric water heater, and crawled back under the blankets. She felt rested and clearheaded. It was obvious to her now that Jonathan's strategy was to drive her away, but it wasn't going to work. He and his money would never separate her from this place and the two people she loved best. But deep inside, she wondered if she had the strength to stand up to him.

She showered and dressed, then, on impulse, put on fresh makeup. No sense in looking the martyr, she told herself, even if she did feel like one.

She let herself into the lodge kitchen where Mike sat at the table talking on the C.B. radio.

"Ten-four. I'll be coming your way this morning. Stand by and I'll give you a call. If you have time, we can have a bit of lunch together."

"Ten-four, Barefoot. I'll be on the by and listening." The girl's voice was soft and musical.

Mike gave Kelly a sheepish grin.

"Is that the new girlfriend?" she asked.

"Sort of."

"What do you mean . . . sort of? What's she like?"

"Well, she's not fat like Geraldine Jenkins!" he said gruffly.

Kelly laughed. "I see you've got all the loot laid out," she said lightly, glancing around the room at the shiny new appliances.

"Yeah. You still mad?"

"No. I don't think so, anyway. I can understand how you and Marty were tempted to take them."

"Oh, that's just great!" Mike got to his feet.

"Calm down," Kelly said quickly. "I said I understand and I do. And, in case you're wondering, I'm not going to let Jonathan Winslow Templeton the Third drive me away from here!"

Mike grinned. "Good girl! I was beginning to think you'd lost your spunk."

"Don't you believe it, buster. I'm as gutsy as ever!" They were brave words, but would she remember them when she faced her husband again?

The test came sooner than she expected.

In the middle of the morning, Marty was in the wash room trying out the new washer when Jonathan's voice came in on the radio.

"Break . . . Mountain View."

Kelly looked dubiously at the set. She desperately wanted to turn it off, but she didn't dare in case of an emergency. She pressed the button on the microphone and said, "Go ahead."

There was silence and then Jonathan's voice. "Will someone bring the truck out to the clearing?"

"Ten-four," Kelly said through stiff lips. She went to get her coat, then relayed the message to Marty, who went to find Tram.

On her way to her cabin, Kelly heard the plane circle to land, but she didn't look skyward. She hated herself for running away, but she needed time to prepare herself for the eventual meeting. Part of her had hoped that, despite the boxes piled in the dormitory, he wouldn't come back. She should have known better, she thought bitterly.

CHAPTER FOURTEEN

WHEN THE FRONT door of the cabin was flung open, Kelly moved away from the chest where she had put away her sweaters and went to stand in the bedroom door. Jonathan glanced at her, then, using the boot-jack beside the door, removed his boots.

"Don't bother taking off your coat and boots. You're not staying." When he didn't answer, she added, "I said you're not staying. This is my house and I don't want you here."

"Who said anything about staying? I came to get my things." He walked past her into her father's room.

"Good." She followed him to the doorway. "The sooner you're away from here, the better I'll like it. Be sure to give me the papers to sign before you leave."

"What papers?" He took his big suitcase from the closet, unzipped it, and spread it open on the bed.

"Don't play games. The divorce papers. You did it all for nothing, Jonathan. I didn't want a settlement when I left you and I don't want one now."

"It was a childish act of vandalism destroying all those clothes."

"They wouldn't have fit Nancy anyway. I didn't want them. All I want from you is the title to this property and I'll keep after you until I get it. I won't let you do Mike and Marty out of their share."

"Didn't they tell you —"

"They told me what you told them," she interrupted coolly. "But I didn't believe it."

He shrugged and dropped a stack of underwear into the bag. "Think any damn thing you please," he said, the words falling icily. "You will anyway. All you know how to do is to break and run."

"What did you expect me to do? Stay and play second fiddle to Nancy?" she almost shouted. "And have that creepy sister of yours look down her nose at me?"

"Watch it, Kelly. Katherine means well. If you'd stayed, you would have seen that I can handle Katherine. But you had to get back here, didn't you? You love this place and . . . Mike and Marty . . ."

"You're damn right I do and you're doing your best to buy them away from me. Can't you be satisfied with what you have? Why did you have to come here and mess up my life?"

"Why not? You sure as hell messed up mine." He stuffed the last garment in the bag and zipped it shut. "I'm staying here, Kelly. You're not going to ruin this vacation for me." He looked at her squarely and she saw new lines of weariness in his face. She was glad if she had pierced his consciousness just one little bit. "I intend to build that glider with Mike and Tram. While I'm here you'd better pull in your horns and act civilized."

"I can't believe you want to stay here! What about the divorce? What about Nancy?"

"What about her? She knows better than to interfere with my plans." He picked up his suitcase and she moved out of the doorway. He pulled on his boots while her mind screamed, *Get out! Get out!* He turned and impaled her with his eyes. "You don't understand one thing about me, do you, Kelly?" His tone was soft, but his frustration was apparent.

Somewhere in a quiet, little corner of her heart she might have felt pity for the man who was so rich in material things and so lacking in what really mattered—love and compassion. But she couldn't close her mind to the memory of Katherine saying, "He didn't want you showing up in Boston."

"I understand enough. Don't come here again." There was a slight tremor when she spoke, but her eyes met his unwaveringly.

"You needn't worry." He picked up his suitcase again. "I brought Bonnie and Clyde back with me. The least you can do is go up there and welcome them back." He went out the door.

Kelly stood in the middle of the room for countless minutes, his words echoing in her mind, his ravaged face fixed in her memory. Was he ill? Stop! she told herself. Stop thinking.

Outside, she was met by an exuberant Charlie with a new red frisbee in his mouth. She took it from him and sent it sailing into the air. Charlie made great, bounding leaps to catch it. He tossed his head, let his toy fly out of his mouth, then pounced on it with his front paws before nuzzling it out of the snow and racing back to her. His big, shaggy body almost upset her when she grabbed the frisbee and held it away from him.

"Oh, Charlie," she laughed. "You're a lover, not a fighter, but that's all right with me."

Inside the kitchen door she stomped the snow from her boots before removing them. "Welcome back, you two."

Bonnie was seated in a wheelchair and Clyde was trying to make coffee in the new electric urn.

"Kelly! You don't know how glad I am to be back here," Bonnie exclaimed. "It's just like comin' home, honey. How y'all been? I worried about you, even if Clyde told me not to." Bonnie's bleached hair was piled high and her makeup was all in place. She looked well-rested and as perky as ever. Her encased leg rested on a prop attached to the chair.

"I missed you, Bonnie. How are you doing, Clyde? You trying to figure out how to operate that thing?"

"We missed you, too," Bonnie continued. "Every day I'd say to Clyde, 'I wonder how Kelly is doin' with the cookin',' and he'd say, 'You just quit your worryin', honeybunch, that gal's been down the trail and she'll manage.'"

Kelly grinned at Clyde. "And I did, Bonnie. My cooking is not up to your standards, but we didn't starve."

"Well . . . ain't ya going to say anything a'tall about all the new stuff?" Bonnie's eyes glittered with excitement. "I tell you, Kelly, I ain't never had such a time in all my life. Clyde said that I ain't better get used to pointin' and sayin' that I'll take this or that. He said it was a once in a lifetime for me, and Clyde's right. It sure was fun."

Oblivious to Kelly's irritated expression, Bonnie continued. "Jack picked up me and Clyde and this here chair and took us down to the department store. Clyde pushed me around and Jack says for me to point out anything I needed out here and not to pay no attention to what it cost. He said it didn't make no difference if it was on sale or not, to get the best. I had those clerks a runnin' in circles! I'd point and they'd jump. I said it wasn't hardly fair for me to have all the fun, but he said you could go anytime you want to get more things." Bonnie paused and waited and Kelly realized she had to say something.

"Good for him," she said, but her sarcasm was

lost on Bonnie, who was off on the description of how they'd picked out the radio antenna.

"Jack said to the man we wanted to listen to the ball games and the man said what we needed was a satellite and we could watch them on TV and Jack said . . ."

Kelly's mind tuned out Bonnie's chatter. Jonathan had won Bonnie over just as he had won Marty and Mike. Damn! Wasn't he going to leave her anything?

"Kelly. Kelly . . ." Bonnie's voice sounded far away.

"Oh, I'm sorry, Bonnie. I was wondering about lunch."

"That's what I said. What should I do about lunch?"

"Mike won't be here. The rest of us can have soup and sandwiches. I'll fix it."

"I'll do it. My arms ain't broke. Help me out of this thing, Clyde. Jack said if I sit all the time I'll lose my figure."

Kelly clenched her teeth. If she heard "Jack said" one more time, she would scream!

The afternoon was one of the longest Kelly had ever lived through. By evening she was so uptight she felt ill. Jonathan spent the day in the dormitory room. "Gettin' settled in," Clyde said as he passed through the kitchen carrying boxes to the shed. Bonnie's exuberance was dampened somewhat when she realized that Jonathan was not going to live in the cabin with Kelly. She continually gave Kelly inquiring looks that Kelly ignored, and after a while Bonnie settled into a gloomy silence.

Sheer willpower and the determination not to let Jonathan intimidate her forced Kelly to remain at the lodge for the evening meal. She was even able to smile occasionally, speak pleasantly when spoken to, and choke down a portion of the food on her plate. Not once did her expression reveal the panic that rose in her throat each time Jonathan looked at her.

The men talked about the glider they planned to assemble and the tower to hold the huge antenna. Jonathan talked easily, discussing ways to fly the machine when it was completed, asking advice, drawing each of the men into the conversation, never once becoming condescending. Marty and Bonnie listened eagerly but Kelly felt like an outsider, excluded.

When the meal was over, the men continued to sit at the table. Kelly and Marty loaded the new dishwasher and made fresh coffee. Kelly put on her coat to take food scraps out to Charlie, then continued down the path to her own cabin. She had never felt so alone or so miserable in her life.

That weekend the retired couple and the two wildlife photographers arrived, and Kelly worked with Bonnie preparing meals. The shed had been turned into a workshop and the big woodburning stove kept it warm enough for the men to work

197

without gloves most of the time. Jonathan spent his days there, coming in with a red nose and, at times, frost on the beard he was growing. He never attempted to speak to Kelly alone and most of the time he ignored her. But it was obvious to Kelly that everyone else adored him.

"I don't understand why you're being so stubborn, Kelly," Marty finally commented. "Why don't you talk things out with Jonathan? I'm sure he'll meet you halfway. You're just making yourself miserable."

Kelly looked at her for a long time, biting back bitter words. Finally she said: "I love you dearly, Marty, but . . . please mind your own business." Tears came to Marty's eyes, but Kelly refused to say more.

The following weekend brought blessed diversion in the form of Andy Mullins, who arrived with another couple, and Kelly's spirits responded immediately to Andy's bouyant personality. He threw his arms wide when he saw her.

"There she is! Ladies and gentlemen, Miss Alaska!"

"Hello Andy. I thought you were going back to the reservation." She held out her hand which he clasped in both of his.

"I called in sick. Told them I had terminal longing to see a pretty girl at Mountain View Lodge." He turned to the couple with him. "Kelly, meet Bob and Maggie."

The woman was a pretty, dimpled blonde with a flawless complexion, who looked at Kelly with disinterest. The man with her was short and stocky and could scarcely keep his adoring eyes from his companion's face. Here was a couple they wouldn't need to entertain, Kelly thought with a twinge of envy. The couple followed Clyde to their room, but Andy lingered with Kelly.

"How are things going with you?" His eyes roamed over her face. "Don't lie."

"Okay. I'm . . . so-so, Doc."

"Did your husband go back to tea-town?"

"No. He's staying here at the lodge. In the dormitory."

"Separated?" He searched her eyes, and she nodded.

"I'm sorry you're so unhappy." His voice dropped to a whisper. "There's nothing I can say, except that the hurt will go away after a while."

"Promise?" Her lips quivered and she blinked to hold back tears.

"Cross my heart and hope to die."

Andy hung his parka on the rack beside the door. "You know something? I like it here. I really do."

"You sound surprised. I think it's Bonnie's cooking you like. Come see her. She's reigning supreme in the kitchen once again."

Kelly held the swinging door open. Andy posed in the doorway, his smiling eyes sweeping the kitchen. "Where's my queen of the cookstove?"

"Andy!"

Bonnie's chair rolled out of the storage room. Jonathan followed behind carrying several canisters. Kelly stood by the door, a fixed smile on her face. Jonathan glanced from her to Andy with a rigid expression and a tiny muscle jumped in his cheek.

"Beautiful as ever," Andy said, taking Bonnie's hands. "And I see you've still got the fellows trailing after you. How are you, Templeton?" He held a hand out to Jonathan. For a second Kelly thought Jonathan wasn't going to take it and the smile slipped from her face. Then, looking as if he detested both of them, he shook it.

"Doctor."

The sound of the deep voice touched something in Kelly's memory, making her heart jump.

"I never got to thank you for sending me that candy, Andy. Or for what you done that day." Bonnie held onto Andy's hand, patting the back of it.

"I'll tell you what," Andy said with a leering grin. "Since I missed out on wrapping up that sexy leg of yours, I'll take a blueberry pie and call it even."

"It's a deal! Push me over to the table, Jack, and I'll get started. Clyde fixed me this here table, Andy. I can get my leg under it and work just fine."

"Is that ugly old Clyde still hanging around?"

Andy teased. "I might have to ship him yet to get you away from him."

"You're a flirt, Andy Mullins. A plain old flirt."

"Shhh . . . Don't tell Kelly. She's suspicious of me as it is."

Jonathan watched Kelly, his eyes shuttered. "I thought you were due back at the reservation," he commented without looking at Andy.

"I got an extension to attend another seminar and come back here to see my girls," he answered lightly. "How's Charlie doing?" he asked Kelly. "Suppose we can hitch him to the sled and go for a ride? I ride . . . you mush."

Kelly laughed. "Oh, no! This is a democracy! We take turns."

"I hate taking turns!"

"Tough! The policy at Mountain View Lodge is share and share alike."

"Not everything," Jonathan said stiffly, bitingly.

Andy seemed not to notice his tone. "I thought there was a catch somewhere," he said gloomily. "Oh, well, if I've got to mush, I'll mush."

Kelly was kept so busy fetching and carrying for Bonnie while she prepared the meal that she didn't have time to think of the conversation until later. When she did and remembered Jonathan's tense words, "Not everything," she saw in her mind's eye a hollow-cheeked figure. Jonathan had lost weight. She hadn't looked at him, really looked at him, for a while. She hadn't noticed before that the work he was doing in that cold shed was taking a toll on him physically. Soon the glider would be ready to fly and he would be leaving. Then she could finally begin to rebuild her life.

"I think that doctor has a crush on you." The meal was over and Marty and Kelly were cleaning up after having sent Bonnie off to her room to rest.

Kelly looked up from scraping food into Charlie's bowl. "Andy is like that with all the women. He just likes to flirt."

"Jonathan didn't like it," Marty said with a warning tone that pricked at Kelly's patience. "I think it bugs him to have men pay attention to you."

"That's too bad! He can shove off anytime he wants. No one's holding him here," Kelly retorted bitterly.

Marty stopped working to look at Kelly with puzzled eyes. "Why do you get so angry? You used to be the most happy-go-lucky person I knew, but lately you're like a bear with a sore foot."

"I'm sorry. I didn't mean to snap."

"Oh, Kelly. Everything would be so wonderful if you and Jonathan could iron out your differences."

"Don't count on it, Marty, because it isn't going to happen."

"Are you interested in Andy?" Marty asked hesitantly.

The simple question sparked an idea in Kelly's mind and she thought a moment before saying, "He's very nice." She allowed her eyes to go dreamy for an instant. "He's nice, he's kind, and he's fun. I haven't had any fun in a long time and I admit I like to be with him."

"I hope that's me you're talking about." Kelly spun around, her eyes wide. "Mike! Stop sneaking up on me!" She moved to hit his arm but he grabbed her hand and twisted it behind her.

"Now, me proud beauty, I've got you in my power," he said in a villainous voice.

"Let go or I'll tell Marty about the girl you talk to on the radio, the one with the melodious voice."

"What girl?" Marty was quick to pick up.

"All right," Mike said, and let go of Kelly's arm. "But you're a killjoy."

"A girl's got to take every advantage she can," Kelly said haughtily, rubbing her wrist.

"Are you man-handling the pretty women, Mike?" Andy asked, coming through the door. "You want me to knock him on his can, Kelly?" he teased.

"Not this time, Andy. I'm afraid he might fight back and I want you to come down to the cabin. I've got a bottle of wine just begging to be opened."

"That's the best offer I've had all day. Hold on till I get my coat and I'll be right with you." He went back through the swinging door and Mike went to speak with Clyde.

"Kelly!" Marty hissed. "Are you out of your mind? Jonathan saw you wrestling with Mike and heard what you said to Andy. He looked as if he could have killed you! He won't like it one bit if you take Andy down to your house."

"Marty, understand this. I don't care what Jonathan thinks. From now on I intend to please myself!"

Kelly and Andy stepped out into the cold night and walked down the path to the cabin. Kelly switched on a light and Andy whistled appreciatively.

"Mmmmm . . . nice! Cozy!"

"Cold, though. Hang your coat beside the door and I'll stoke up the fire."

"Let me do it," he offered and set the firescreen aside. He knelt down in front of the fire to prod the glowing embers with a fire tool. "I can think of better ways to keep warm," he grumbled.

"I just bet you can," Kelly laughed. "How about a hot buttered rum? That should warm you up."

"If that's the best offer I'm going to get, I'll take it."

"You're not nearly the wolf you pretend to be, Andy Mullins. If I said, come on, Andy, let's go to bed, it would shock you to death."

"Maybe, but I'd die happy."

Kelly felt laughter bubble up in her. "Poor, deprived Andy. I bet you have all the Indian maidens on the reservation coming to your clinic with every excuse from hangnail to heartburn." She set out mugs and put the kettle on to boil. "I'm sure I have a bottle of rum around here somewhere. There it is on the top shelf. Will you get it down, Andy?"

Andy came up behind her and reached for the bottle, his other hand resting on her shoulder. Kelly didn't hear the door open, but she felt the cold draft. Looking under Andy's arm she saw Jonathan standing in the doorway. He stared at her in silence, then shut the door and took off his coat.

Andy's hand squeezed Kelly's shoulder in conspiratorial understanding. She knew she would have to say something.

"We're having a hot rum, Jonathan. Would you like one?"

He strolled toward them, a tall, taut figure, maddeningly in control of himself. "I'll have mine straight," he said, getting out a glass.

"There's whiskey, if you'd rather have it," Kelly murmured.

"This will do fine." He poured himself a drink, gulped it down, and poured another.

Kelly's heart sank as she saw how much he was drinking. He swallowed it rapidly, his fingers tight around the water glass. She mixed the hot drink for herself and Andy, handed the glass to him with a forced smile, then went to stand beside the fire. Andy followed.

"I'd like to be here when you take that glider

up," Andy said. "Mike mentioned your plan to try her out next week."

"It'll depend on the weather," Jonathan replied and the look he flashed at Kelly was as brief as lightning and just as searing. He stood beside the kitchen table, the rum bottle in one hand and the water glass in the other.

Andy made several more attempts to keep the conversation going which Jonathan answered as briefly as possible. Finally Andy set down his mug and went to get his coat.

"Thanks for the drink, Kelly. I'd better get back up to the lodge or Maggie and Bob will think I've deserted them."

"I'm glad you came down, Andy. We'll do it again, soon." The smile stayed on her face, although her muscles were aching from the strain.

As soon as the door closed behind Andy, Jonathan set his glass down on the table with a crash. "So, were you going to take him to bed?"

"And if I was? What business is it of yours?"

"I'll tell you what business it is of mine," he shouted. His hands closed roughly on her shoulders and his dark eyes burned into hers. His fingers moved to her long bare throat. "You're my wife, damn you! No man touches my wife, but me!"

He dragged her to him, his mouth bruising her lips, his arms hurting her. He seized her dark hair in his hand and pulled her head back, then kissed her hard and long, his lips forcing her own to part so his tongue could plunge and probe.

She fought him with all her strength. She would never respond to him in this mood. If only his lips would soften, if only he would show some tenderness. He flung her onto the couch and stood over her with clenched fists, his face contorted with fury.

"I could kill you, Kelly! I don't want to hurt you!"

She looked up at him, white and trembling. "Please go."

He nodded wearily, his eyes flashing with shame and self-contempt. "I'm sorry," he whispered.

In a few quick strides he had plucked his coat from the rack and disappeared into the cold, dark night.

CHAPTER FIFTEEN

THE MEN CARRIED the glider out of the shed, unfolded the brightly colored wings, and snapped them in place. Kelly had looked forward to, yet dreaded, this day. It was midmorning. There were several hours of sunlight left in the clear, cloudless day. Clyde started and restarted the motor, while Tram buckled Jonathan into the folded canvas chair suspended from the aluminum frame. Kelly stood beside Marty, silently watching

Jonathan. An almost breathless feeling came over her, an urgency to beg him not to go up in the flimsy contraption. He didn't look at her and when he put a crash helmet on over the ski mask he was wearing, he looked like an astronaut preparing for blastoff. The men gathered around him, as excited as small boys, giving advice, wishing him luck, telling him not to damage their toy.

"Are you going to wish him luck?" Marty asked. When Kelly shook her head, she added, "Well, I am!" She ducked under the wing and placed her hand on Jonathan's arm to get his attention. "Good luck, Jonathan. Be careful. Don't get to thinking you're a bird up there and land in the trees."

He lifted a mittened hand and waved. The sight sent new dread shooting through Kelly.

Then the roar of the snowmobile drowned out any other words. The chain link between the aircraft and the snowmobile tightened and the glider began to move. Mike would tow it out to the clearing, then pull it into the wind. When the plane was airborne, Jonathan would release the tow rope. He planned to circle the area several times, keeping the resort in sight.

In a matter of minutes the glider and the snowmobile were out of sight. Kelly heard the roar of the engine as the machine picked up speed, then the orange, green, and yellow wings of the glider appeared like a giant butterfly above the trees.

Jonathan was up there! The thought struck Kelly like a physical blow. She closed her eyes, not daring to look. When finally she opened them again, Jonathan and the giant wings looked like a large bird in the sky. He circled and passed over them and headed toward the mountains. Suddenly the small purr of the motor died and there was silence.

Everyone strained to hear the engine start again. "Start it, boy . . . start it," Clyde mumbled aloud.

The silence was deafening. "What's happening?" Kelly's voice was so loud it shocked her. "What's wrong?"

"The motor cut out on him, but he can ride on the current until he can get it started again," Tram said calmly.

"But if he can't get it started again . . . he'll crash!" Her plaintive voice and anguished eyes begged Tram to tell her it wasn't true.

"What do you care?" Marty said cruelly. "You wouldn't even wish him luck."

"Hush up!" Tram said sharply. Marty burst into tears and ran for the lodge.

Kelly scarcely knew when Marty left them. Her eyes were glued to the speck in the sky that was getting smaller and smaller. Mike roared away on the snowmobile, and as Kelly stood numbly, Clyde backed out the truck, paused long enough to pick up Tram, and drove away.

"What good is the truck?" Kelly shouted. "You

can't go cross-country!" She ran toward the cabin. "Don't let him crash! Please don't let him crash!"

Minutes later she was loading the sled with blankets, a first aid kit, whiskey, a battery light, and survival supplies. She had often seen her father aid stranded motorists or hunt for a lost tourist and she knew what to take. She was wearing her down-filled snowmobile suit. "Always take more warm clothing than you think you'll need," she remembered him saying. She grabbed her fur parka and two sleeping bags, and called to Charlie.

"Come on, boy. It's up to you and me . . . or Mike. Those two greenhorns in the truck will never find him." She talked softly to the dog, who stood patiently while she fitted his harness. "We'll take your new frisbee along, Charlie. See, I'll put it here on the sled where you can turn and see it. Let's go, Charlie. Jonathan is somewhere out there and he could be hurt! Mush . . . mush!"

Charlie was delighted to be pulling the sled. He took off across the snow, past the kennel of yipping huskies, without giving them a glance. Kelly ran along behind, holding the handles. Once she'd been able to run several miles before hopping onto the sled runners, but after they passed the grove and were halfway across the clearing, she had to rest and let Charlie do the work. Keeping her eye on the spot on the horizon where she had last seen the glider, she kept Charlie moving, although she knew he was tiring. She strained for the sound of Mike's snowmobile, but there was only silence.

Kelly was reasonably sure Jonathan would try to come down before he reached the mountains. She remembered hearing him say, "Lean forward and the glider goes down, lean back and it goes up. It's the shifting of your weight that controls it."

The wind picked up, stinging her face, and she pulled the ski mask down over her cheeks and nose. Gray clouds came rolling in from the north and the sky that had been clear a few hours ago was suddenly dull. Kelly pulled Charlie to a stop to allow him to rest and decided to put on the cross-country skis attached to the back of the sled. After that, the going was easier, but she looked at the sky with worried eyes and tried not to think about Jonathan lying in the wreckage of the glider. Doggedly she kept going, every step taking her farther and farther from the resort. Several times she blundered into a snowdrift. Often she was tempted to stop and rest. But soon the first intermittent snowflakes began to fall, and within fifteen minutes huge, fluffy flakes were falling fast. Worried that she wouldn't be able to see the wreckage of the glider, Kelly began calling out a "Ha . . . looo," a long high shrill sound that she knew carried on the brisk wind.

She looked at her watch and was surprised that she and Charlie had been traveling for almost two hours. It would be dark soon. She was frightened, so frightened she thought she would be sick, but she kept moving and calling. Once her voice cracked and she thought she couldn't continue. Charlie howled.

A stabbing pain in her side forced her to stop for a moment. She thought she heard a faint sound, and lifted her cap from her ear to listen. Nothing. She let go with a long shrill "ha . . . looo," and waited anxiously. The sound that floated back to her was indistinguishable, but definitely human!

"Mush, Charlie. Mush . . ." she shouted, directing him to the right. "Ha . . . looo, ha . . . looo," she called into the near darkness. The answer became clearer, and she followed the sound, her heart beating a rapid tattoo of relief.

"Here . . . here . . ."

Charlie saw him first and barked his pleasure. Then Jonathan materialized out of the snowstorm, standing beside the glider, his helmet in his hand and his ski mask off. Snowflakes stuck to his dark beard. He grinned broadly at her and she threw herself into his arms, crying hysterically. The force of her weight knocked them both to the snow. Jonathan gave a surprised gasp:

"Kelly! For heaven's sake. Kelly!"

It hadn't occured to her that he wouldn't know the person calling was her. Now he lifted her ski mask and held her close against him.

"You fool girl! Whatever possessed Mike to let you come out in this storm?"

"Mike had nothing to do with it, you idiot! Whatever possessed you to go up in that awful thing? You scared the hell out of me! I wish you'd broken your neck!"

Jonathan's laugh rang out, and he nuzzled her warm face with his cold one. "No, you don't! Shhh . . . Stop crying. . . . You were worried about me? You cared? You love me . . . that much?"

"I don't even like you!" she shouted against his neck, but she was hoarse from calling out to him and the words came out in a croak.

Jonathan sat up and pulled her up with him. "Are you all right?"

"I'm hoarse, you . . . flying turkey!"

"Do you think if I kiss it, it will make it well?" he asked huskily.

As they sat in the snow, the heavy flakes threatening to cover them both, Jonathan pulled her onto his lap and cuddled her close. Warm, firm lips found hers and he kissed her softly, tenderly, lovingly. She didn't want to cry again, but she was so tired. They sat there for a long time, his arms tight around her, not speaking, merely needing the closeness and security of each other's bodies.

"What do we do now, my little Sherpa of the mountains?" he whispered. "If we sit here much longer, we'll be buried under the snow."

Kelly moved out of his arms and looked about. She could barely make out the shape of the glider.

"How did you get down?"

"I found a smooth spot and came down. Worked great!"

"Great, my fanny! If it worked so great, why didn't you bring it back home?" she said crossly.

"I tried, sweetheart. I really did, but the wind was all wrong."

"Come on, Charlie. We could set a match to the silly thing, but Mike wouldn't be able to see a house afire in this storm," she grumbled.

"Kelly!"

"Just hush up, Jonathan! I'm so mad, I might just hit you! Fold up the wings on that thing and we'll use it for shelter. It's not good for anything else."

She unpacked the sled and unharnessed Charlie. "I'm sorry I didn't bring you anything to eat," she told the dog.

"What about me?" Jonathan said. "I'm starving."

"Then starve. I'm still mad!"

Kelly turned on the battery light and unfolded a thin nylon tarp which she spread over the wings of the plane.

"Scoop snow up on the ends and tramp it down," she instructed, then covered the snow beneath the tarp with a ground cover before throwing in the blankets, sleeping bags, and her fur-lined parka. After turning the sled up onto its side, she crawled into the shelter. "It isn't home, but it'll have to do until it stops snowing and we can shoot off a flare."

"A flare?" Jonathan asked, crawling in beside her. "What else do you have in that Girl Scout pack?"

"Chocolate, raisins, and whiskey."

"No TV dinners?" he teased.

"What did you expect? I didn't have time to pack a picnic lunch. I was scared out of ten years growth!" Her fingers were shaking as she tried to take the top off the whiskey flask. Jonathan laughed and she snapped, "You act as if you're on a holiday! You fool! Didn't you know you could have been killed out here?"

"I was almost at the point where I didn't care. Now, I'm grateful to be alive! Take a drink of that whiskey, darling. You're going to need it." He moved closer to her but she leaned back.

"Stay away from me, Jonathan!" She couldn't see his face in the darkness, but she knew he was smiling. "Stay away, or I'll make Charlie bite you!"

"Charlie wouldn't do that." The dog heard his name and tried to sneak into the shelter. Jonathan rubbed his nose. "Lie down, boy. See, he likes me," he said arrogantly.

"He wouldn't if he knew you like I do."

"What do you mean by that?" All teasing was gone from his voice.

"Just what I said. I'll be truthful and admit that when I thought you had crashed, my heart almost stopped beating. But that doesn't mean I'll live with you. Frankly, I don't like you, Jonathan."

"What have I done to deserve this dislike?" His voice came quietly out of the darkness.

"How can you even ask such a question?" she demanded wearily. Their body heat was warming the shelter and she took off her cap and mittens.

"We've got to have the truth before we can understand each other, Kelly." She was silent. "Let's start with . . . Boston. I was too possessive of you, wasn't I?"

She gave a groan of despair. "I don't want to talk about that."

"We must, darling. I've had plenty of time to think about it. I realize now that I acted out of jealousy. I was eaten up with it." The words came out reluctantly. "I wanted you to be so completely mine that I smothered you."

"Jonathan . . ."

"Let me say this because I may never have the courage again. As soon as I took you to Boston I knew it was a mistake. I forced you into a new environment before you had even gotten used to me. But I wanted you with me so badly I didn't care. I didn't want to share you with Katherine, or Nancy, or any of my friends. I didn't want you to have anyone in your life but me. I hated Mike and Marty because they had a piece of your love and I wanted it all. I was actually glad when you didn't like Nancy or Katherine."

"Your own sister?" She was aghast.

"It's contemptible, isn't it? Do you think I

wanted to feel like that? I couldn't help it," he said harshly. "You'd fallen in love with me without knowing I was a Templeton of Boston. I was thrilled with the idea that you loved me and not the man with the name. I can't remember when I felt loved, or even liked, because I was me."

"How can you say that? Katherine loves you."

"Katherine loves the Templeton name, the Templeton traditions. I'm merely the vehicle for carrying on those traditions. She doesn't care about me as a man. It took me a while to figure that out, but now I know it's true." His voice was hoarse with emotion.

"Why didn't you tell me this before?"

"I have my pride," he spit out. "I didn't think you would understand. You had Mike and Marty. I had only you."

"But when we went to Anchorage . . ."

"I was in heaven . . . then hell when you came back here without me. Why didn't you wait for me at the apartment?"

"You set me up! Why did you send me there knowing Katherine and Nancy were there?"

"I didn't know they were there until I got to the office. They'd only arrived the day before and Mark tried to tell me at the airport, but I was so anxious to be alone with you I wouldn't listen."

"Katherine implied they had been there for a long time. She said you found the apartment for them so they could make . . . social contacts for you."

"She lied," he said flatly. "When I went to the apartment and found her there, I told her to butt out of my life and take Nancy with her."

"She said you were going to marry Nancy before Christmas."

"Never!"

"She said you didn't want me to come to Boston to get my things, that I had embarrassed you enough. She said . . . no implied . . . that you were making love to me in order to lower the settlement you feared you would have to pay to get a quick divorce. She offered to buy me off."

"Oh, I'm sorry, darling. No wonder you left as you did! I thought you wanted to get back to be with Mike. I was so jealous . . ." He put his arms around her and drew her to him. "Forgive me, darling. Please forgive me and . . . love me."

"I still love Mike and Marty, Jonathan. Not the way I love you, but you must understand I won't exclude them from my life." She rubbed his furry cheek with her fingertips.

"All right. Actually, lately I've had the feeling they like me, that they would accept me into the family, in spite of the Templeton name."

He lowered his head to kiss her and Charlie let out a fierce growl. Startled, they broke apart. The dog stood in a taut stance, the hair on his back straight up. Gutteral noises came from deep in his throat. Kelly reached for the light and shined the beam out into the darkness. Two red eyes gleamed back at them. Charlie lunged toward the animal and the red eyes disappeared. Kelly and Jonathan waited tensely and presently Charlie returned to stand in front of the shelter.

"What was it?" Jonathan whispered.

"A wolf." Kelly laughed softly and switched off the light. "Wait until I tell that smart-aleck Mike that the dog he gave away is a great sled dog and a fighter, too! Charlie would have tackled that wolf! Good boy, Charlie. Remind me to buy you a new ball."

"I bought him a new frisbee."

"Playing up to my dog! I ought to give you a black eye!"

Jonathan laughed. "If you're going to do it, get it over with so we can get into that sleeping bag. I've never slept in one before. Will it be warm enough without these suits?"

"We won't know if we don't try it, will we?"

They snuggled down in a single bedroll, the blankets and fur parka over them, their legs entwined as intimately as their arms.

"I feel as if we're in a cocoon. I'm as warm as toast."

Kelly giggled. "Why not? You've got all that whiskey inside you."

"And you on the outside. Mmmm . . . your mouth tastes like chocolate."

"There's some left. It's there beside the lamp."

Jonathan lifted his head. "Charlie's eating it.

That's okay, Charlie," he called, "I've got all I need, right here." Soft arms wrapped around his neck and she rubbed her cheek against his. "Do you mind the beard, sweetheart," he asked against her lips.

"I love it. Kiss me, Jonathan."

His lips hovered. "Not Jack?"

"I've got Jack out of my system. It's Jonathan I love. For too long I loved two men. Now I've settled on one."

"I love you, sweetheart. Stick with me and help me learn to share you. It won't be easy for me. I never believed you cared for me the way I cared for you. From the day we met, I wanted to put you in my pocket and keep you all to myself. I know now that I was crushing you, killing that beautiful spirit that flows from you and touches everyone around you." He stroked her lips with a tenderness he had never shown before. "I'll make it up to you, darling."

"It wasn't all your fault, Jonathan. I had a dream of a prince sweeping me off my feet and our living happily ever after in his castle. I should have tried harder to understand you and convince you that I loved you. We'll have to work hard to stay together. Love alone isn't enough."

"We'll never go back to Boston, darling. I never want to see that sad, haunted look on your beautiful face again," he muttered thickly, his lips nipping at the smooth line of her jaw.

"We have to go back," she said firmly, her hand against his cheek. "Don't you see, darling? We can't solve a problem by not facing it."

"I don't want to go back. I've never been so content in my life as I have been here in your home, even though my jealousy was eating me alive. I love it here. I've already taken steps to move my headquarters to Anchorage. We may have to go back to Boston for a month or two, but that's as long as I want to stay. We'll build our life here."

Kelly almost burst with joy at knowing how much he cared for her. She held him to her with all her strength and murmured soft words of love against his lips.

"I've missed you horribly, my only love. I never again want to spend a single minute away from you. Hold me and love me."

His mouth closed fiercely over hers, parting her soft lips, urgent in his need. Her body felt boneless as he fitted every inch of her against him. She could feel his powerful body tremble with desire, and she moved her stocking foot up and down his muscular calf.

"Damn, damn . . . underclothes," he muttered. "They should be banned." His hand fought its way under her shirt.

"In Boston?" she giggled.

"Everywhere! Darling, I've got to have you!" His mouth devoured her softly parted lips and her senses soared under the slow, sweet arousal of his caress. "I don't suppose you brought the . . ."

She pulled back. "Of course not!"

"Would you be terribly unhappy if we . . . if it happened?"

"No. Would you?"

"I'd love to have a baby with you. What better way to hold you to me than to keep you barefoot and pregnant?"

"Jonathan!"

"I'm kidding, sweetheart. Remember that boy we met in the doctor's office? The one who wanted me to tell my kids not to ride on the handlebars of the bike? Well I want one like him . . . but I'll take what I can get. A boy and four girls."

"Four girls?"

"Well . . . three?"

"Two! And that's my final offer!"

"I'll take it!"

Center Point Publishing

600 Brooks Road • PO Box 1
Thorndike ME 04986-0001 USA

(207) 568-3717

US & Canada:
1 800 929-9108
www.centerpointlargeprint.com